WRATH

OF

The Reapers

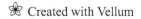 Created with Vellum

CONTENTS

Dear M, M, & T
Thank you for always believing in me, even when I
couldn't believe in myself.

PLAYLIST

Angels Like You by Miley Cyrus
Only One by Yellowcard
Beggin For Thread by BANKS
Ghost by Justin Bieber
HAUNTED by Isabel LaRosa
Horns by Bryce Fox
Leave Out All The Rest by Linking Park
The Devil by BANKS
Witness by Rosie Darling & Rajiv Dhall
How Long by Tove Lo

TRIGGER WARNING

The Reapers are not good men. They have no moral code and they certainly have no limits. If you're looking for a story where the heroine turns the bad boys good, well then this story isn't for you. This is the world of The Reapers and the only way to survive is to play by their rules.

The Reapers of Caspian Hills is a Dark Romance and features content that some readers may find disturbing. Visit the author's website for a detailed list of potential triggers and as always, reader discretion is advised.

This is book is dedicated to my ride or die readers. Here's to all of us finding our happily ever afters.

PROLOGUE

Stevie

EVERY VILLAIN HAS AN ORIGIN STORY. AND DESPITE what most fairy tales lead you to believe, most villains aren't born evil - *they're made.* They start out as regular people, living their lives day to day like you and me, until one day something happens. Something that breaks them. Something that changes not only the way they view the world, but the way they view themselves. They transform into someone else entirely and the person they were before becomes nothing more than a memory. A haunting reminder of what could've been, had things played out differently.

The Reapers were supposed to be the villains in my story. They were the ruthless mafia brothers who pumped our city full of drugs and ruled the streets with an obscene amount of cash and a shit-load of violence.

When I first came to them, I was nothing but a toy. A new shiny object for the big bad wolves in designer suits to play with. They could use and abuse me as much as they wanted, and I knew no one would step in to stop them. There was no hero waiting in the wings. No knight in shining armor coming to my rescue. I was on my own, and the only way I was ever going to make it out alive was if I played by their sick and sadistic rules.

And I did, for the most part. Until the lines between hate, lust, and love started to blur.

Atlas, Ezra, Tristan, and Cyrus understood me more than anyone else ever has. They embraced the darkness. The ugly twisted parts of my soul I've spent my whole life trying to hide, and not only did they accept me, they loved me.

For a moment, what we had was perfect. The fairy-tale ending I never saw coming.

But the universe had other plans.

With a strike of a match, everything, and I mean everything, I had built with The Reapers, went up in flames. The love. The trust. The loyalty. All gone.

I tried so hard to salvage what I could from the ashes, but with more questions than answers from the men I thought I knew, I didn't know who to turn to, let alone who to trust.

Lies were told, promises were broken, and mistakes were made. And honestly, I have no one to blame but myself for what happened.

Every villain has an origin story, and this... *is mine.*

ONE

Stevie

THE AIR IS DIFFERENT IN THIS PLACE. STAGNANT AND thick. Laced with this underlying scent of decay that only years of neglect could bring. It's hot and impossibly humid too. I woke up a few hours ago with a parched mouth and nearly every inch of my body coated in a thin layer of sweat.

It's dark. So purely pitch black that it's almost impossible to see anything in front of me. It's the kind of darkness nightmares are made of. The kind of darkness you can't stare at for too long, not without panic setting it.

What is this place?

From what I can tell, I'm not injured, and aside from the tight ropes biting into my ankles and wrists and the pounding headache that still hasn't gone away, I feel little pain.

I have to give it to them. Whoever tied me to this chair knew what they were doing. I've been testing the binds since I woke up and all I've managed to do is rub my skin raw.

I'm not sure how long I sat here drifting in and out of sleep before I came to. Minutes? Hours? Days? My memory is hazy and the longer I sit here, the harder it is to keep track. I don't know what Dimitri wants from me or why the hell he's left me here. *All I really know is I need to get the hell out of here.*

THE NEXT TIME I wake up I try to search the darkness again, but there's still nothing discernible about this place. Just four dark walls cast in even darker shadows.

Staring out into the void feels like I'm drowning. Like I'm sinking beneath the depths of thick, murky water and no matter how hard I try to claw up to the surface, I can't. There's no light to guide me. Just darkness. All-consuming, inescapable darkness.

I should be used to this feeling. I think bitterly as I give up on the search and close my eyes once more.

I've been drowning for a while now. In guilt. In fear. In emotions I was never really equipped to handle. And being in this place only seems to amplify that feeling. Almost as if the dark solitude is forcing me to face everything I've been trying to avoid.

I'm not a good person. I used to think I was, but after everything I've done, how can I possibly still believe that?

My little sister is dead because of me. Ezra may have been the one to pull the trigger, but Alex would've never been on his radar if I didn't selfishly put her there.

Same with Melanie and Charles. They were the closest thing I had to friends, and they died trying to save me from a lunatic I stupidly lured in. The Reapers warned me about Dimitri and I always knew there was something off with him. I was just too selfish and bullheaded to see how dangerous he was until it was too late.

I've hurt the people closest to me and if my dad were alive, he would be so fucking disappointed in the person I've become. Cold. Ruthless. Deceitful. That's not the kind of woman he raised me to be. Then again, maybe that's the biggest problem in all of this.

I've spent my whole life trying to be good and live

up to the standards my father set for me. But maybe I've just been fighting a losing battle all along. Maybe hurting others is in my DNA. *After all, I'm not just his daughter, I'm hers too.*

TWO

Stevie

A FEW DAYS LATER

I'M DRIFTING. Floating somewhere between being asleep and awake when I hear the distinct sound of the lock on my door shift. It's a tiny disruption. One I probably shouldn't notice. But I've always been a light sleeper and being in this place has trained me to stay vigilant.

I keep my eyes shut as the overhead lights flicker on and the door slowly creeps open. Pretending to sleep never stops them, but I'm greedy for any moments of reprieve I can get.

"Good morning." A chilling voice calls out, cutting into the silence that normally fills the room. Even without looking, I know who it is. Dimitri's right hand man, or as I like to refer to him as, The Zombie.

I'm sure he has a real name, one Dimitri's called out on more than one occasion, but I refuse to learn it. Fuck humanizing the enemy. Besides, learning anything else about him feels a little morbid considering I plan on slaughtering him.

The Zombie's footfalls are slow and methodical as he approaches me, almost as if he's purposely taking his time to scare me, but I stuff the fear down before it can take root. *He's not worth it.*

"I know you aren't sleeping." He taunts, stepping deeper into the basement. "If I'm honest, I couldn't sleep either. I stayed up all night thinking about you."

His little confession makes me want to gag. Having him visit me is bad enough, but just the idea of this sick fuck thinking about me on his downtime makes me want to scrub my skin off.

He stops moving, and for a moment; the silence is deafening. I try to listen for him, but the only sound coming through is the rhythmic pounding of my own heartbeat.

"Open your fucking eyes." He snaps, reappearing within inches of me.

Before I can even think about following his orders, he latches onto the back of my head and pulls. Yanking my hair back so violently that it feels like my scalp is literally being ripped off.

I don't scream, because fuck giving him the satisfaction, but the sudden burst of pain is blinding. I have no choice but to move to relieve some of the pressure.

I try to inch closer to his hand, but the ropes around my wrists keep me practically glued to the chair and I have no choice but to sit and wait until he's done for the pain to stop.

I've lost count of how many times he's greeted me like this in the last few days. Three times? Five times? Nine? It's hard to discern one memory from another in this place.

"You have no one to blame but yourself for that." He says as he finally loosens his hold and relieves some of the pressure. "Now how about you be a good girl and do as I ask?"

Begrudgingly, I force my eyes open and glare at the monster standing above me. *Jesus.* I don't think I'll ever get used to seeing him this up close. I nicknamed him The Zombie for a reason. The man looks like Dimitri ripped him out of a fucking horror movie, and not the psychological thriller kind, the gory, gives-you-night-mares kind.

His shiny bald head gleams under the fluorescent light and his sickly pale skin is so thin it's almost transparent. He has over-exaggerated features that only add to the air of otherworldliness about him, with cold, lifeless eyes, a prominent nose, an oversized mouth, and jagged, silver scars covering nearly every inch of his skin. He cocks his head as he takes stock of me, a cold chill instantly climbs up my spine. *I hate the effect he has on me.*

"I said good morning." He hisses, gritting his teeth as he glares down at me. "It isn't very polite of you not to say anything back."

I almost scoff at his words. He wants *me* to be polite? He can't be serious.

I blink at him, like he's the stupidest person I've ever met, because, well he just might be and his lip curls in response.

Wow… he isn't kidding.

I guess it makes sense considering how deranged his boss is.

Dimitri swears his intentions are pure. That he orchestrated all of this, not to punish me, but to help me see how *generous* his offer is. He's convinced I'll come to thank him for this in the end. Now, if that doesn't speak to how delusional the man truly is, I don't know what will.

"What's the matter?" The Zombie asks, grabbing

ahold of my face and letting his hot breath dance across my skin. "Cat got your tongue?"

He painfully squishes my cheeks together, using his filthy fingernails to dig deeper and deeper into the skin until I have no choice but to pry my mouth open and relieve the pressure.

"Nope." He says, staring at my tongue with a smirk. "Still there."

He runs his thumb across my bottom lip and I dig my nails into the arms of my wooden chair to stop myself from repelling. "It would be a shame if your bad attitude forced me to cut out that pretty little tongue of yours."

He's bluffing. Dimitri lets him get away with a lot, but he'd never let him cause me any permanent damage. Not because he cares about me, but because if I agree to his offer, I'll need to look like I'm doing so willingly. Cuts and bruises can heal in a few days, but anything more severe will raise some serious red flags.

I can't smell much of anything, thanks to the mixture of blood and sweat permeating in the air, but I make a show of dry-heaving from the stench of his breath just to fuck with him. It's juvenile, but part of surviving means doing whatever I can to get under his skin. After all, every second I'm in his head is a second he isn't beating into mine.

"You think you're funny?" He snaps, practically snarling the word at me, as if doing so will somehow scare me into answering him.

I can't help but laugh as I lick at my cracked lips. *Actually, yeah.* I think I'm pretty hilarious. All things considered.

He cocks his head at me, like he's actually expecting an explanation, and my laughter only grows. *What part of I'm not fucking cooperating are you not getting?*

I feel the sting of my lips splitting, but I can't stop. It's just so fucking ridiculous. *Look at me.* I'm bruised and beaten. Covered in a mixture of dried blood and my own filth because I'm refusing to comply with their demands. What the hell makes him think that this interaction is going to be any different?

Without warning, his fist strikes out, smashing into the side of my face with enough force to break skin. My head painfully jerks to the side and a familiar burn ignites across my cheek as the fresh taste of copper fills my mouth.

Fuck.

He continues his assault on me, like a rabid fucking animal, and I wish I could say I'm surprised at how hard he's hitting me, but I'm not. After spending so much time in this place, I've learned there's nothing Dimitri's men love more than making me bleed.

I know I should stop this. I should just give in and avoid all of this pain. But I can't let Dimitri win. *I won't.*

After a while, his blows lull to a stop and he backs away to assess the damage. "My, my, my…" He says, smiling down at me. "That looks like it hurts."

I can't see the damage he inflicted but I can feel it. The left side of my face is throbbing and I can already feel my eye swelling shut, but it's my head that I'm really worried about.

The torture sessions with him are always bad, but they never leaving me feeling like this. I must've really pissed him off this time and if I don't do something to stop him, he's going to kill me. Intentionally or not.

I release a whimper and force myself to start crying, doing what I can to attract his attention. It's calculated, but it's the first sign of defeat any of them have seen since the torture sessions started. Instead of being suspicious, like he should be, he looks at me and his face is practically beaming with delight.

"Are you finally ready to agree?" He asks, cutting right to the chase. "We're just getting started, but it doesn't look like you can handle much more."

I give him a small nod and keep my head low, playing up my defeat to the fullest.

He immediately jumps into action. He whips his phone out and when I see him dial a number and press the phone to his ear, a hint of a smile plays on my lips. *Good boy.*

He mumbles out a few Russian words I don't understand as he paces back and forth. And just as quickly as he started the call, he ends it.

For a while it's just the two of us, and even though my head is down, I can still feel his eyes on me.

Studying me, like he's still not quite sure if he believes me. It's too late for him to change his mind. The call's already been made.

A few moments later, the door slides open and another person enters the room. They don't say anything as they take their position behind me, but their notable silence tells me everything I need to know. *It's Dimitri.*

Dimitri and his men have been trying to break me for days. Rotating shifts every few hours to torture me, feed me, and escort me to bathroom in that order. Ironically enough, Dimitri only shows up to feed me, so the fact that he's here now means my shitty acting actually worked.

"Speak." The Zombie says, his voice laced with pride. "We don't have all day."

I slowly nod my head and gesture for The Zombie to come closer. Like the coward he is; he looks to Dimitri for permission before making a move. It's hard not to laugh at the irony. He wants permission to approach me, but beating the shit out of me without so much as a warning is a-okay.

Dimitri gives him a firm nod and, like the perfect little lap dog he is, The Zombie eagerly approaches. As I watch him move towards me, I can almost see his thoughts written all over his face. He thinks he's won. That all of his violence has finally forced me to comply, and damn, does it make me giddy just thinking about how wrong he is. *Enjoy this moment of bliss, you stupid fuck.*

As soon as he's perched beside me, I make a move to speak. I can even feel the phantom words dance on the tip of my tongue, but instead of uttering the words of agreement both of them are desperately wanting to hear, I gather all the blood in my mouth and spray it, splattering bloody saliva all over the side of his face.

I watch with wild amusement as he implodes. His entire body vibrates with the need to hurt me and it's obvious he's seconds away from losing it.

I laugh, because I can't help it, and the sound of my laughter only seems to fuel his rage. His head snaps up and the look on his face is the most sub-human thing I've ever seen. He wants to kill me, I can see it in his eyes and fuck, it feels good to know I'm the one who's pushed him there.

Looks like I broke you first, asshole.

Within seconds, Dimitri is between us, acting as a human shield as he shoves his rabid henchman away. To anyone else, his actions would look heroic, like a small part of him cares and wants to protect me. But that's just another one of his illusions. I've spent too much time in this place to mistake his interference as anything other than an act of self-preservation.

"I'm sorry to waste your time, boss." The Zombie huffs, speaking to Dimitri as he continues to glare daggers at me. "I thought I had her."

Dimitri shakes his head slowly before palming the man's blood-splattered face in his hands. "You did good, Ivan." He assures, releasing his hold as he leads him towards the exit. "This one just needs a little more convincing than most. But she'll break. Eventually, they all do."

I narrow my eyes at him, but say nothing as I watch his henchman quietly exit the room.

The door closes, and part of me knows I should feel better. The Zombie was on the verge of killing me, and I should be relieved that he's gone. But when I look at Dimitri and see the strange gleam in his icy blue eyes, I know the real torture is only beginning. I'm not sure what he's planning, but one thing's for sure... *this is going to be a long fucking night.*

THREE

Stevie

"KROSHKA, WHY MUST YOU BE SO DIFFICULT?"

Dimitri cocks his head as he perches beside me, almost as if he actually doesn't understand my logic. "This could all be so much easier if you just agree."

I stone my features and stare off into the distance. We aren't having this conversation again. What Dimitri wants me to do *will* hurt The Reapers. I don't care how I left things between them, no amount of "convincing" will ever make me agree to that.

Like the manipulative asshole he is, Dimitri whips out a silk napkin from his pocket and starts dabbing at the fresh blood seeping from my cheek.

He's showing me kindness and a week ago, I would've eaten that shit up. I would've searched his eyes for some sign of remorse and when I saw some intangible sign he cared, I would've excused his behavior. Brushed it off as a weird miscommunication. But the veil over my eyes has been lifted, and now I can see Dimitri for who he truly is. A fucking monster.

Dimitri places his hand over mine and looks up at me with pleading eyes. "All I'm asking for is your hand in marriage."

He drops to one knee beside my chair, and I have to physically restrain myself from showing the repulsion that surges through me.

"I want to give you a beautiful life. Is that so wrong?"

It's a lie.

"You will want for nothing," he continues, squeezing my hand tighter, "and I will protect you and yours better than The Reapers ever could. I know the situation is not ideal..." He pauses, mostly for dramatic effect. "But what beginning ever is?"

He looks deeply into my eyes and the fact that all I

see is emptiness staring back at me makes my skin crawl. *He's such a wolf in sheep's clothing.*

"Think of your sister..." He continues, moving his hand down to my thigh before squeezing my knee. "Don't you think after everything you've been through, she'd want you to be happy?"

Happy. I think, shaking my head with a bitter smile. *God, does he really think I'm going to buy this?*

He always does this, acts as if he's done nothing wrong. As if he has my best intentions in mind and his altruistic approach is simply being misunderstood.

I watched him brutally murder Melanie and Charles with my own eyes. That doesn't just go away. When I can sleep, the image of blood pooling around their lifeless bodies still creeps into my nightmares.

He can try to disguise his intentions all he wants, but it's clear that this proposal has nothing to do with me. It's about *him* and his incessant need to one-up The Reapers.

I haven't spoken a single word since arriving here, but I'm so sick of his manipulations. Of his lies. And just hearing him talk about my sister so freely like that pushes me over the edge.

"Fuck you." I snap, narrowing my eyes at him. My voice is rough and scratchy from the days of misuse, but the message is clear enough. "You don't get to speak of my sister. Not now. Not ever."

My words waver from all the pent up rage, but I don't stop. He needs to get this through his thick fucking skull and if I have to spell it out for him, so be it. "I will never agree to be your wife." I add, looking him up and down in disgust. "You could offer me the world and I'd still say no. You and I both know where my loyalty lies."

Dimitri's nostrils flare as he takes in my venomous words. It's obvious he wasn't expecting such a harsh refusal, but that just goes to show how little he knows me.

"Your loyalty." He scoffs, flinging his soiled napkin to the ground. "How could I possibly forget about that? All they've ever done is cause you pain, and yet there you are, clinging to their sides like a pathetic puppy."

Dimitri paces, glaring over at me as his anger intensifies. "There's a fine line between loyalty and stupidity, Kroshka. Tell me, what has all of your loyalty given to you? Hmm? You have no friends. No family. No one left that gives a single fuck about you."

His words hurt more than I expect and, as numb as I want to appear, I can't help but avoid his gaze. *I don't want to think about that.*

"Where are your men, Kroshka?" He taunts, looming over me like he's seconds away from biting my head off. "By now, they know of Melanie's death. My people had time to discard the footage of our unfortunate encounter, but once they found the bodies, it would only take a quick surveillance search to see you were there with her. They know you're missing, yet they haven't bothered to look for you. Why do you think that is?"

I feel my throat bob and the sudden urge to run barrels into me. I don't need to hear this. He's just trying to manipulate me.

"You don't actually believe they still care about you, do you?"

The silence that falls between us is deafening, and I can almost feel the heat of his stare as he scrutinizes my expression. Trying my best to remain perfectly unaffected, I continue staring off into the distance. I know him. If he sees any signs of my pain, he'll pounce.

"You do." He says flatly, glaring at me like the mere sight of me makes him sick. "Don't you understand? You were nothing to them. A toy. Nothing else. Those men are incapable of loving anyone but themselves. Their absence alone proves that. I am the only choice you have left."

Dimitri could be right. In fact, a big part of me fears he is. But that doesn't change how I feel about them. *How I'll always feel about them.*

Love is funny that way. Once it's there, it's almost impossible to get rid of it. It doesn't matter what was said, or how badly the ties were severed. When you truly love someone, you love them for a lifetime.

I love them. Regardless of whether or not it's reciprocated. Regardless of what happens next, I love them, and a part of me always will.

"You'll never be my choice, Dimitri." I say simply. "And you're right, they may not want me. But that doesn't change the fact that I'll never want you. You can try to manipulate the truth all you want. How I feel about you will never change."

Dimitri stares at me, holding my gaze for longer than anyone should. I feel uncomfortable under the weight of his stare, but something about the look in his eyes keeps me locked in place.

"It's a shame it had to come to this." Dimitri murmurs, shaking his head with a sigh. "I thought with enough force, you'd agree and I could spare you, but it seems you're too stubborn for your own good. I offered you another option out of the kindness of my heart, but in truth, I never needed your hand in marriage. You've only been gone a few days and already The Reaper's crowns are tarnishing. It won't be long until their loyal subjects turn on them and they lose everything. Congratulations Kroshka, you've finally accomplished what dozens of men have tried and failed to do. You crumpled their kingdom.""

Whatever he has planned won't be good. I can sense it in the way he looks at me. Like deep down, he pities me for what he was about to do.

"Sleep well, Kroshka." He calls over his shoulder as he heads for the door. "Something tells me you're going to need all the rest you can get."

I cling to my detached expression like a shield of armor as he walks out of the room. The lights shut off and after he closes the door behind him, I'm in the darkness once more.

He's going to kill me. I think to myself as I clench my jaw and shove the storm of emotions trying to come to the surface back down. *I've refused his proposal and now he's going to kill me.* I think again, sinking my teeth into my bottom lip. *Why wouldn't he?* I'm worth more dead to him than I ever would be alive.

I really fucked up this time, didn't I?

It's ironic. Every choice I made was to protect the people I cared about, and in the end, I still ended up losing everything.

Maybe all of this was inevitable. Part of some grand scheme already written in the stars. I loved, I lost, and now I'll die because of my choices. I can live with that. Well, I guess, die with that.

FOUR

Stevie

I AWAKEN TO THE SMELL OF GASOLINE PERMEATING IN the air. It's everywhere, suffocating me to the point where it's almost impossible to breathe. *What the hell is happening?*

I force my eyes open, but the fumes are so strong that I only manage to blink a few times before the stinging sensation slams them shut again.

"There she is." A muffled voice murmurs from somewhere close by. It takes a second for me to place his voice, but once I do, the fine hairs on the back of my neck stand straight up. *Dimitri.*

He brushes a few stray hairs from my face, and the panic within me heightens. *He's come to finish what he started.*

I knew this was coming. I sat in the darkness for hours, imagining this moment. Trying to prepare myself as best as I could for what he was going to do. But thinking about it and actually experiencing it are two very different things. *I'm not ready to die.*

"Shhh." He whispers, grazing his rough fingers down the side of my face. "There's no need to cry."

Am I? I can feel a lump in my throat and a slight tremble in my body, so I must be.

I take in a few slow breaths, doing what I can to calm myself down, but with him this close to me and the sharp scent of gasoline lingering in the air, it's almost impossible to relax.

All my mind can seem to focus on is the fear of what's going to happen next.

"Poor, Kroshka." He says as he brushes his fingers through my tangled hair. "You had so much potential, but you couldn't see beyond your loyalty. It's a shame I have to do this."

I snap my eyes open and glare up at him. "Then don't." I choke out, wincing as the fumes make my eyes water even more.

I can't see his full expression through the gas-mask he's wearing, but I can see the amusement in his eyes clear as day. He didn't expect that.

Taking advantage of the window, I continue. "Let me go and we can pretend like this never happened. I'll disappear and the effect will still be the same. No harm, no foul."

"No harm, no foul, huh?" He asks, holding my gaze. "What about The Reapers?"

"What about them?" I ask, shaking my head as I clench my jaw. "I had time to think about it last night, and you're right. They don't want me. Everything they've done until now proves that. It would be stupid of me to go back to them and honestly, all I really want is to start over and put all of this shit behind me."

Dimitri studies my face as if he's searching for some kind of sign of deception. He won't find one. I told the truth. *Mostly.* It *would* be stupid of me to go back to them and I do want to start over. He just doesn't know that I've never had a problem with doing stupid shit for the people I love and that the only people I'd ever want to start over with are them.

"It's a tempting offer." He muses as he paces back and forth. "It would save me a lot of trouble, and I have always had this strange fondness for you. It would be a shame for you to die so young."

Yup. Such a shame. So, let's not do it.

"Then again," He says, cocking his head at me. "Your plan has one fatal flaw."

I furrow my brow. *What flaw?* I told him everything he wanted to hear.

He watches me as he lets the words slowly tumble from his lips. "I wouldn't get the satisfaction of watching you burn."

Dimitri grabs a red canister and douses me in gasoline. I gasp in horror as the icy cold liquid splashes across my skin and soaks my stained white dress, making the thin cotton fabric cling to my body.

"What the fuck are you doing?" I scream, feeling the panic inside of me explode out. "Don't do this Dimitri. Please, please don't fucking do this." I'm sobbing now. Hiccuping between shuddering cries as the terror takes hold of me.

"You feel it, don't you?" Dimitri asks, studying me. "That your death is near. I wonder if she felt it too?"

I blink my tears back and stare at him. "Who?"

Dimitri scoffs, as if it's the most ridiculous question he's ever heard. "Your sister, of course. I couldn't be there when my men killed her, but I wonder if her cries sounded just like your's."

His words jar me so violently that it takes a few seconds to recover. *He didn't kill Alex. He couldn't have.* I vehemently shake my head, as if doing so will make my thoughts more concrete. "You're lying." I hiss, glaring up at him. "You didn't even know my sister."

I tilt my chin up indignantly to mask just how much his words affect me. *He's a liar.* It's what he's good at. Why should this time be any different?

Dimitri glares at me, and it's obvious he's enjoying every second of this. "I understand the confusion. All the evidence I planted pointed to Ezra, but I did worry that you wouldn't buy it. You were so much smarter than I expected, but I suppose, in the end, you weren't smart enough."

A flood of emotions swirls inside of me, and it's nearly impossible to keep my composure. I want to scream and cry and kill that asshole for killing her. For letting me believe for even a second that The Reapers had something to do with her death. *Why would he kill Alex? What fucking purpose would taking my little sister's life serve?*

The moment the answer hits me, my mouth goes dry. *Me.* He took her to get closer to me. To drive a wedge between me and my men. If Alex weren't missing, would I have ever trusted that bastard? *Fuck no.* He knew the only way to get close to me was to take something important from me and place the blame on the men I love.

A mixture of rage and shame blossoms in my gut. *How could I be so stupid?* How could I ever trust him? How could I ever think Ezra would kill her? All he's ever done, all *they've* ever done, is try to protect me. And what did I do in return? I fought them. I hurt them. And I betrayed them. It's no wonder they haven't come for me. *Why would they?*

"Why?" I ask, wincing at the sorrow laced in my voice. I know the answer, but the sick masochist in me wants to hear it from him. "Why did you kill her?"

"You know why." He retorts, cocking his head at me. "Without her disappearance, I would've never been able to get close to you. Her death was unfortunate, but necessary."

I glare at Dimitri and am thoroughly disgusted with what I see. There is no kindness in his icy blue eyes. No hint of humanity. Nothing.

"What do you want with The Reapers?" I ask, tired of his games. "You barely know me. There has to be more to this for you."

Dimitri laughs as he slowly circles around me. "That is the age-old question, isn't it?" He muses. "I hate to disappoint you, but I don't want anything. Wanting leaves room for disappointment. So no. I don't want. I take. I force. I consume. I don't want anything from The Reapers, but I will take everything from them. Starting with you. So I'll ask again, one last time. Agree to be my wife or die an excruciating death. The choice is yours."

Every single cell in my body wants to explode on him. To lash out and throw everything I have at the asshole. But I stop myself short.

Reacting without thinking is what I always do. It's what led me down this path of destruction and, ultimately, it's what brought me here. If I want things to play out differently this time. If I want to avenge my sister and save myself, I need to stop and think for once.

Dimitri has the upper-hand, and even without these ropes on my wrists, he and I both know my hands are tied. If I agree to his proposal, I'll never be free of him. I'll be forced to live a lie with a man I despise for the rest of my life and have to constantly pine for the four men that truly have my heart. If I deny his proposal, he'll set this place on fire and I'll die down here. But it'll be on my terms and I'll no longer be a pawn in his fucked up little game.

So I choose the only route that I can choose. The only choice that feels right in the sea of past fuck-ups that brought me here.

I choose to burn.

FIVE

Stevie

Sweltering heat licks at my skin and it already feels like I'm boiling from the inside out. The smoke hasn't reached me yet, but I'm sure it won't take long for the fire to spread. The asshole coated this place with enough gasoline to fill up a cruise ship.

Once I gave him my answer, Dimitri didn't say a word. He simply held my gaze for a few seconds. There were no more taunts from his end or questions. He just stared at me with the bitter look of disappointment in his eyes before he finally walked out the door.

I think at that point; he knew there was no use trying to talk me out of it. I had made my decision, and I was ready and willing to die with my choice.

After he walked out, I thought for sure he'd start the fire down here and cut right to the chase. But I should've known better. He wants to punish me, and the best way to do that is to draw this out for as long as possible. Force me to feel every ounce of terror I can as my death slowly draws near.

I look and watch with a mixture of fascination and horror as dark wisps of smoke climb across the ceiling. It won't be long before the flames come. It's only a matter of time.

I hear the faint rumble of an engine roar to life before slowly fading away. It's Dimitri, it has to be. I guess he's decided to flee the scene early. It makes no difference to me either way. I'm already dead in every other sense of the word and it's a smart move on his part. A fire of this magnitude won't go unnoticed, no matter how hidden this place is.

Smoke engulfs the room, making every breath I take thicker and thicker by the second. I'm going to pass out

There's something strangely calming about accepting your death. I don't know what happens next, but for once in my life, I don't feel the need to. I guess that's the rainbow at the end of the tunnel for me. For these last few moments of my life, I'm not scared anymore.

I close my eyes and visibly swallow as the heat intensifies and when I try to adjust in my chair, my slick hands somehow slip out of their binds.

The irony is a tough pill to swallow, but instead of thinking about the what-ifs, I simply fold my hands in my lap and try to fight the urge to run.

It's too late to do anything about it, anyway. The only viable exit is puffing out enormous clouds of dark smoke and if, by some miracle, the flames don't kill me, the smoke definitely will.

"Hello." I hear a feminine voice call out, accompanied by the sound of loud banging. "Hello!" They try again, sounding almost frantic. "Is there anyone in there?"

My eyes flash open, and I frantically look around the room, trying to find the source. "Yes!" I scream, as a whole different kind of fire ignites under my ass. "I'm here!"

Instead of wasting time freaking out about the miracle of all miracles happening to me, I take action. With my hands now free, I bend over and rip the fuck out of the binds around my ankles. They're tight too, but they're no match for my slim fingers and my will to survive.

"Listen to me." The voice calls out. "We're going to help you get out of there. But the entire place is on fire.

You can't get out the way you came in. You'll have to use the stairs."

"What stairs?" I call out, scanning the dark room for any sign of them. I had no idea there were even stairs in here.

"Follow my voice." The girl says. "There should be a set of stairs somewhere in there. And hurry. We don't have anything to put out the flames and the fire is spreading really fast."

Fuck. If it reaches this room, I'll be scorched in a matter of seconds.

"I see it." I screech, taking the steps two at a time as I rush towards the freedom that didn't seem possible thirty seconds ago.

I make it about halfway up the rickety wooden stairs when the room below erupts in bright orange light and the roar of fire blocks out everything else.

Shit.

I make a mad dash for the set of double doors above me, using every single ounce of energy I have left to get me to the top of those stairs.

"We can't open it from this side." The girl says, somehow still holding my attention even as the room below me erupts in chaos. "You're going to have to unlock it from your end."

The smoke is everywhere, and it's burning the hell out of my eyes. Pushing through the pain, I throw my hands against the doors and start blindly searching for the latch. As soon as my fingers latch onto the cool metal, I do everything I can to pry it open, but it's no use.

"It's locked!" I shout, coughing as the smoke surrounds me. "I can't open it."

"Vi, we have to go." A masculine sounding voice calls out. "The cops will be here any minute."

"She can't get the latch open." The girl screams back, sounding almost as desperate as I feel as her words get lodged in her throat. "It's locked. You guys have to help get her out."

"What's the holdup?" Another voice asks, laced in . Hearing the clear annoyance in his voice makes me second guess everything.

Wait. Who the hell are these people and how did they even find this place?

It's the first time I've questioned any of this, but the coincidences are piling up.

What if this is some kind of trap?

A booming sound shifts my attention to the center of the room and I stare in disbelief as a huge wood beam comes crashing down to the floor. Pieces of cinder and ash fly into the air, coming dangerously close to me, and I instinctively scream at the top of my lungs for help.

I don't give a fuck if this is a trap. I need to get out of here. *Now.*

I hear one of her friends offer her words of comfort while another one steps in. "Stand back!" He shouts. "I'm going to kick the door open."

I heed his warning, even as the flames lick up the stairs and black soot starts to coat my skin. There doesn't seem to be any gasoline up here, but because Dimitri doused me in it, I'm still only seconds away from being lit up like the Fourth of July.

With three solid kicks, the double doors burst open and a set of powerful arms throws a large hoodie over me before pulling me to safety. I don't have any strength left to react. I just flop limply in his arms and pray like hell that I've made the right choice. I don't even know who these people are, but something in my gut tells me I'm safe and as the last bits of my consciousness slip away, and the darkness pulls me under, I cling to that thought and that thought alone.

SIX

Violet

"JESUS CHRIST, SHE SMELLS LIKE GASOLINE."

My head snaps up at Rome's sudden outburst, and I give him a sneer. I knew it was only a matter of time before he said something. He's been silently brewing ever since Niko loaded her into the back of his precious Range. I know how particular he is about his things, so I even went through the trouble of laying a tarp down to protect his interior, but it's obvious he still isn't happy.

47

As much as I dislike how rude he's being right now, I can't argue with him. He's right, she does smell.

In the short time we've been on the road, her nauseating scent has already permeated throughout the SUV. I'm not sure how she managed to climb up those stairs without succumbing to dizziness. Just being in the car with her is disorienting enough.

I roll my window down to air it out some, but it does nothing to soften Rome's deep scowl. He'll just have to get over himself. She needs us and there's nothing wrong with being a good person every once in a while.

"At least that lets us know it wasn't an accident." I say, shrugging my shoulders. "They left her there on purpose. They wanted her to die down there."

"Good observation, Detective V." Dallas teases, as he bumps his huge shoulder into mine. "The real question is, why?"

I wince a little as I rub at the bruise I'm sure is bound to form on my shoulder. Dallas isn't doing it on purpose, but I swear sometimes he forgets that I'm not one of his six foot tall friends built with a physique of a linebacker.

I glance back at the girl in question and try to discern anything I can while she's still passed out. She's laying in a fetal position and the hoodie that Niko threw over her is covering almost all of her body. I didn't recognize her voice from the club. Then again, she did kind of sound like she swallowed a chainsaw whole, so I have no idea what her real voice sounds like. I don't know who she is, but she must have done something stupid to wind-up in Evanoff's house. No one just accidentally stumbles into a place like that.

"Does he ever have a reason for doing what he does?" I ask, mostly to myself. I've witnessed some of the cruelty that goes on in Evanoff's clubs and I know the things they do to the girls are never justified. Torture is a turn on for those sick men.

"In his mind he does." Niko huffs, gazing out the window in the passenger seat. I'm mildly surprised he's even paying attention to the conversation. He always seems like he's on another planet.

"So, what do we do now?" Dallas asks, "About the girl, I mean."

"Maybe we should just drop her off at a hospital?" I suggest.

"We can't do that." Niko retorts, shaking his head. "We have no idea if he has eyes there and if he finds out she survived, he's going to want to know who helped her."

I give him a nod, already understanding where he's going with this. We can't take her to a hospital, not unless we're willing to risk the possibility of exposure and give up on everything we've been working towards. "Rome, what do you think?"

Rome releases a long sigh as glares at me through the rear-view mirror.

"I don't know, Violet." He glowers, narrowing his

eyes at me. "None of this was part of the plan. We were supposed to go after Evanoff, but someone decided her bleeding heart was more important than everything we've been working towards. Now he's gone and we're stuck having to clean up his mess."

"She was in danger." I say, trying to defend my decision. I shouldn't have jumped out of the car without telling them. I know that. But once the flames started, I had this sinking suspicion that he'd left someone inside and I couldn't leave them there to die. "We made the right choice."

"Vi, we don't even know who this girl is, let alone if she can be trusted." Niko says, turning around to face me. "For all we know, she earned her execution."

"No one deserves to die like that." *No one.*

I can't believe he and Rome are being so dismissive about someone's life. Then again, I shouldn't be surprised, it wasn't that long ago they faced a similar decision, and if it wasn't for Dallas, I'm sure I wouldn't even be here right now.

"Bad things happen to people all the time, Violet." Rome adds, throwing metaphorical salt in my wounds. "We can't go around trying to save everyone. Especially when we don't know who they are or who they're connected to."

I let the conversation end on that note. I don't have any more energy left in me to argue with him.

He's right. I can't save everyone. I know that better

than anyone. But I can't help but feel proud of what we did back there. And as much as he doesn't like what happened, he can't deny the fact that he played a big part in rescuing her, too. For all of his grumbles and groans about wanting us to stay out of it, when I needed his help, he was there for me and that's something I didn't expect from him.

I AWAKE with a jolt as the car pulls to a stop and my eyes fly open. Immediately, Dallas's hand is on mine, squeezing it tight and whispering reassurances in my ear. I'm not sure how he could pick up on my panic so quickly, but I'm relieved nonetheless. I scoot closer to him and nestle my face against his side.

"Damn it, V." Dallas jokes, shaking his head. "You better quit touching me like that before I'm tempted to make an honest woman out of you."

The southern drawl in his rich voice puts a smile on my face and I purposely slip my arm around him and squeeze tighter. He's joking. Obviously. We're just friends, but I refuse to stop touching him on principle alone. "Admit that you're in love with me and I will." I prod, pressing my face against his side to stifle my laugh.

Dallas says nothing in response and when I look up

at him, there's a little less amusement in his eyes than there was a second ago. "Alright, V." He says, shaking his head with a smile. "Enough jokes. Rome and Niko already went inside and I need to pee like a racehorse. It's time to get your lazy ass up."

I must've drifted off while we were driving, because when I sit up and take a look outside, I see that the scenery surrounding us has changed. Evanoff's kill house was located deep in the woods and the last thing I remember seeing was a long stretch of winding road lined with tall eucalyptus trees. Now we're in the middle of civilization. There are strip malls on every corner and the gas station we're parked at is bustling.

"Where are we?" I ask, raising my arms and pulling them into a long stretch.

"Just outside of Caspian Valley." He offers. "We got a tip that Evanoff was heading back into the city, so we're going to head there."

I give him a nod as I slowly rub my eyes and let out a long yawn. I'm a lot more tired than I thought and the fumes filling the car probably didn't help. I chance a glance back at our stow-away. *Poor thing.* She's still passed out and probably will be for a while.

"Come inside with me." Dallas says, grabbing my attention as he lingers just outside of his open door. "You can caffeinate and stock up on all the junk food your little body can handle." He says, wiggling his brows. "My treat."

I throw him a broad smile and slide out to join him.

One of my favorite things about Dallas is that he never makes me feel weird about money or my lack thereof. I'm sure he's noticed by now that things always seem to be "his treat" but he never makes me feel bad about it. He acts as if I'm the one doing him a favor, which is as ridiculous as it is charming.

After loading up on snacks and taking the longest pee of my life, Dallas and I head back to the car and find Niko and Rome already ready to go in the front seat.

"All set?" Rome asks, as Dallas and I slip into the back seat.

"Yup," Dallas retorts with a nod, "and... we brought snacks."

Without warning, packs of gummy candy and chips start raining down in the front seat. I noticed he bought way more than we needed for one stakeout, and now I know why. I have to stifle my laugh as two most stoic people I know sit there silently as bags and bags of snacks bounce off of their heads.

Then the bickering starts.

I still can't fully wrap my head around how these three became best friends. They're all so different from each other, but I guess theirs is a bond that doesn't really need to make sense. It just is.

I had a bond like that, too. Once. In another life.

I turn to grab my seatbelt, and when I notice a discrepancy, I stop in my tracks.

"Uh, guys?" I ask, turning around to eye the space behind me. "Where is she?"

Their bickering dies down as all of their heads snap towards me.

"What are you talking about?" Rome asks, furrowing his brow. "She should be right there."

"Well, she isn't." I explain, turning back around to face them. "She's gone."

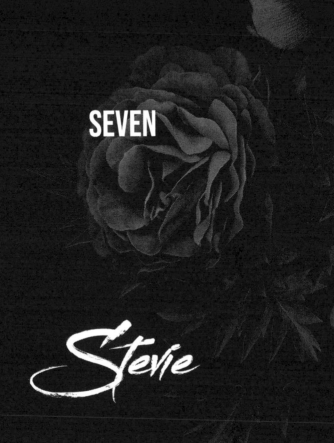

SEVEN

Stevie

THE SMELL OF HOT ASPHALT AND BURNT RUBBER STINGS
my nose as I lay flat against the warm pavement and wait
for them to leave. I've tucked myself between a couple
of parked cars on the opposite side of the parking lot, so
I'm at a safe enough distance where they shouldn't spot
me, but I can't be too careful.

From this vantage point, the cars I'm nestled between
obstruct most of my view, but from what I can tell, all

four of them have already made it back to the car. *So, why the hell haven't they taken off yet?*

When I slipped out of the trunk, I didn't really have a plan in mind. I just knew that this could be my only chance to escape them and I needed to take while I still had the chance.

They may have saved my life, but it's clear to me that the people in that car are dangerous. I was falling in and out of sleep for most of the drive here, so I didn't hear every conversation they had, but the ones I did pick up on raised some serious red flags.

Just like I had initially thought, they weren't at that house by happenstance. They were there with purpose. They've been following Dimitri for weeks. Tracing his movements up and down the coast. Tonight was the closest they've come to catching him and they would have succeeded had I not thrown a wrench into their plan.

I don't know why they're after him or what they plan to do to him once they get him, but I don't really need to know. The fact that they're involved with him tells me everything I need to know. They can't be trusted.

Someone opens their door and my breath catches.

Fuck. Fuck. Fuck.

I can't see who it is, but I can tell by the smaller size of their boots that it must be the girl. *Damn it.* She must've realized I left.

Her feet turn into a slow circle and even without

seeing her expression, I can tell that she's looking for me.

I hold my breath as she moves to scour the parking lot and when I see someone else step out of the car to join her, I roll myself under one of the cars.

Fuck. They aren't going to let this go, are they?

After a few minutes of searching individually, the man joins the girl. I can't hear exactly what he says to her, but whatever it is, it's enough for her to give up the search and climb back into the car with him. I relax a fraction when I see their doors close, but it isn't until they pull the SUV back onto the road that I let myself breathe a sigh of relief.

One problem down, a million more to go.

COLD WATER DRIZZLES down my face, leaving my skin streaked with long dark lines of remnant soot. I dip my hands under the faucet again and splash some more, wincing a little as the icy water hits my tender flesh.

After drying my face with the roughest paper towel on the planet, I stare at my reflection in the mirror and can't help but grimace at what I see.

The dirt may be gone, but I still look like shit.

It's the first time I've been able to get a good look at

myself in days. And even without examining the rest of my body, it's painfully obvious that Dimitri and his men did a number on me.

My face is red and swollen with blotches of deep purple and bright red bruises littering most of the left side. There's a gnarly gash on my cheekbone that looks like it's going to need stitches and my lips are so scabbed, it hurts to move them.

Most of my injuries look worse than they feel, but it's my eyes that really concern me. They're empty and cold, as if I lost the last bits of my humanity down in that hell hole.

Maybe it did.

I hear someone coming towards the restroom and I immediately snap my head down and pull my hood closer. *I don't need to attract anyone's attention right now.*

A girl walks through the door and I can just make out her silhouette as she steps up to the empty faucet beside me. She looks to be around my age and from what I can tell, she's dressed in black from head to toe. Her hair is tucked securely under her hoodie, but when she pulls her sleeves up and leans over the sink, I spot a curtain of long lavender hair slipping over her shoulders.

"Why did you run?" She asks, her voice only slightly louder than the water that's splashing over her hands.

I chance a glance at her, but only catch a glimpse of

her profile as she turns away from me to soap her hands. "Excuse me?"

"You left." She clarifies, keeping her head down as more of her lavender hair falls into her face. "I'm curious why. You know you're safe with us, right?"

"Oh." I say, choking a little on my words. *They came back for me. Why in the hell would they come back for me?* "Look." I breathe as I grab a paper towel off of the dispenser beside me. "I appreciate what you did back there, but I'm better off on my own."

"No, you're not." She says, twisting to face me. "No one is."

The minute our eyes lock, my eyes flare and we both do a double take.

No. I think, shaking my head. *It's not possible.*

The girl's name was Violet. *Not Alex.* I have to be imagining this. Or weirdly superimposing Alex's face on her.

I look into her eyes and, to my surprise, recognition as clear as day shines in her eyes.

She knows me.

"Alex." I hesitate, breathing the word out as if doing so will make the question less impactful.

It's not her. It can't be.

"Jesus, Stevie." She curses, shaking her head as her hand reaches out to graze my face. "That was you in there? God, what did they do to you?"

She pulls me in for a hug, but I still don't know how

to react. My body just seizes up like a statue as her long arms wrap around me and my vision starts to blur.

I'm imagining this. I have to be.

"Stevie?" She asks, pulling back to get a better look at me. "What's wrong?" Her brows knit together as she studies my battered face and even more tears well in my eyes.

"You aren't her." I hear myself whisper as a lone tear spills down my face. "You can't be. Dimitri killed her."

"Stevie, look at me." She says, placing her hands on my shoulders and peering into my eyes. "I am her. Dimitri doesn't know what the hell he's talking about. He thinks he killed me, but he's wrong."

"You're Violet." I say, shaking my head. "Not Alex. I heard them say it."

She jerks back as her brow furrows into a scowl. "It's an alias. I use it to protect myself."

I shake my head as I bite down on my lip. I'm still having a hard time wrapping my head around this. *Alex is alive. Alex is fucking alive.* "Why didn't you tell me it was you?" I ask, glaring up at her.

"I didn't recognize you." She says, backing away from me as she softly shrugs her shoulders. "Or your voice. The thought never crossed my mind that it was you. You weren't even supposed to be there tonight."

My eyes grow wide at her words. "How the hell would you know that?" I ask, backing away from her as I cock my head. "Did you know where to find me?"

She averts her eyes. "Stevie, this whole thing is a lot bigger than me and you. It's not that simple."

"Answer the question, Al." I snap, blinking back my tears as the emotions inside me slowly transform into anger. "Did you know how to find me?"

"Yes." She says defeated as her shoulders slump. "You were supposed to be at The Diaz Estate."

What the hell? Why does she know so much and where the hell has she been?

"Why didn't you contact me?" I ask, my voice thick with emotion. "I looked for you. I..." I hesitate, shaking my head as I clench my fists. "We looked for you. Why didn't you tell me you were okay?"

"I couldn't." She says, averting her eyes as she shakes her head. "You don't think I wanted to? It's complicated and it's a long story."

I cross my arms over my chest and clench my jaw. "I've got nothing but time, little sis." I say, glaring at her. "Explain."

Alex's mouth forms into a hard line as she tilts her chin up. "Look." She asserts, holding my gaze. "I'll explain everything when we get in the car. But not here. Now, come on. The guys are waiting."

I begrudgingly follow her to the car, purposely dragging my feet just to grate on her nerves. She turns to check on me and I immediately flip her off, feeling just as satisfied as I do stupid for being so immature about it. Never one to let a dig slide, no matter how petty. Alex bends her elbows and raises both of her fists before knocking them together a la 'friends' style, and I have to bite back the urge to smile at her. I'm still pissed at her, but I can already feel my anger subsiding. No matter what mistakes led the both of us here, she's still my little sister and I'm grateful as hell to have her back.

EIGHT

Violet

"Do you think she's having a stroke?"

I scowl at Dallas and jab my elbow into his side. "That isn't even funny to joke about." *She isn't having one.* At least, I don't think she is. Though I am starting to grow a little concerned.

She hasn't said a word since Rome stopped speaking. She's just sitting there, staring into the fireplace.

Niko walks into the living room carrying a plate

stacked with sandwiches and a few bottles of water tucked into the crooks of his elbows. He sets everything down on the coffee table between us and takes a seat beside me on the couch. "I take it she still hasn't said anything yet." He says, cocking a brow at her before glancing at Rome. "Maybe you broke her."

Stevie snaps her head up and levels her eyes on us. "I'm not broken." She says, narrowing her eyes at him. "Or having a stroke. I'm just... processing."

I can't blame her. What we just told her is a lot to take in. I mean, even I still have a hard time wrapping my head around it and I've had weeks to adjust to the news.

Dimitri Evanoff is a DEA agent.

I don't think anyone would've seen that coming.

"He works for the good guys..." Stevie says, pulling her brows together in a scowl. "How the fuck does a monster like that work for the good guys?"

"For the record, good and bad is subjective, Big Sis." Dallas says, flashing her a smile as irritation flickers across her face. "The police aren't always good and criminals aren't always bad."

"Thanks for the life lesson, Cowboy." She deadpans, rolling her eyes. "And stop calling me 'Big Sis'. I barely know you."

Having had enough of their bickering, Rome breaks up their conversation and cuts right to the chase. "From what we've been able to gather, he started out as an informant when he was around eighteen years old. Giving them tidbits of information here and there to keep up appearances and earn the DEA's trust. Once he was officially employed with them, the boy scout routine went out the window. He still works for them, but now he only acts with his own interests in mind."

"Sounds familiar." Stevie says pointedly as she clenches her jaw and glares at him.

She's still angry at them for keeping me hidden. It's obvious. But she seems to have an even deeper hatred towards Rome. She hasn't said why, but I know my sister well enough to know why she has a grudge against him.

Ever since I can remember, Stevie's always been very 'black & white' about things. In her mind, there is no gray area. Either you're right, or you're wrong. She trusted him to do a job, and he failed her. I'm sure the reasoning behind her hatred is as simple as that.

But things are a lot more complicated than what they appear to be and the conversation we're having right now is just the tip of the iceberg.

Stevie crosses her arms over her chest and looks away. She wants to stay angry. I can tell. It's why she hasn't even touched the throw blanket Dallas gave her, even though her body is literally shivering.

Stubborn freaking mule.

She shifts in her seat and tries to be nonchalant about it, but I notice the way her eyes linger on the plate of sandwiches.

"Eat." I say, shoving the plate towards her. Her eyes snap towards me and there's a sadness there that I didn't expect. She's visibly upset and showing it so freely like that is so unlike the Stevie I know. "I know you're hungry. You exerted a lot of energy back there and we don't need you to pass out on us right now."

Logic always outweighs emotion with her and if we want her cooperation, that's how we'll have to approach this.

Stevie reaches for a sandwich and I breathe out a silent sigh of relief. She takes a few bites and picks up the conversation with The Mercenaries again. "So if he's been working for the DEA since he was eighteen, then this isn't just about The Reapers." She says, reaching for one of the water bottles. "It's about The Organization."

"We think so." Rome says with a nod. "Which is how we became so involved in this. We've been working with The Organization for years, taking care of their more unofficial business needs. Once we found your sister and realized Evanoff was involved with her disappearance, we knew we needed to look into everyone involved before moving forward."

"And that's how you found out he was a spy." Stevie adds, slowly nodding her head as the pieces of the puzzle click into place.

"Yeah. That was something we didn't expect." Niko says, shifting forward in his seat to grab a sandwich of his own. "He's been with them so long, The Organization should've detected it sooner, but there was never a reason to suspect him of any foul play. On the surface, he was the perfect soldier."

"So, what does The Organization plan to do with him? I'm assuming you guys told them what you found."

"We did. We presented everything to them and when the subject of outing him for being a spy came up, they took it very seriously. They even brought it to a vote. But two of the five council members voted against it, and any action they take has to be unanimous, so it died there."

"What?" Stevie asks, incredulously. "But he's literally working against them. Why would they do that?"

"Because for them, image is everything." Rome says, shaking his head. "They'd rather let Evanoff wreak havoc in his bubble than admit to the world that they put a fucking DEA agent in a position of power."

"And the other three?" She asks. "What about them?"

"Their hands are tied." Niko answers. "They can't "officially" do anything."

"But they can, unofficially hire you guys." She says, shifting her eyes between the three of them. "So that's why you've been tracking him."

"Yup, for the last couple of weeks we've been hunting him down." Dallas says as he slowly pulls the crust off of his sandwich. "Mother fucker is impossible to keep eyes on."

"Yeah." Stevie agrees. "He has a way of popping up in the most unexpected places and then disappearing without a trace for days. Now it all makes sense. He's been playing both sides all along."

"Which is why he needs to be stopped. Now that he has power within The Organization, he's already starting to implement changes that The Organization doesn't condone. Changes that, if reported to the authorities, will get syndicate leaders like The Reapers some serious fucking jail time. Not to mention hurt a lot of innocent people.

"Like what?" She asks, shifting her eyes between the three of them.

"Like human trafficking." I say, holding her gaze. "That's what I meant when I said this whole thing is a lot bigger than just us. If he pulls this off, we're talking about hundreds of innocent people getting hurt. We can't let that happen."

Stevie chews on her lip as she studies me, searching my eyes as if they'll show her something if she looks into them long enough. She hasn't said anything, but I can already hear the words before they form on her lips. *What happened to you?*

I know I'm eventually going to have to talk to someone about what happened, but I also know it can't be her.

How do I tell my sister that the men sent to kill me, decided to sell me to traffickers instead? How do I tell her that those traffickers were even more depraved than the bastard we're hunting? How do I tell her that by the time The Mercenaries found me, Alex was dead and I had transformed into someone else entirely? The answer is simple... *I don't.*

Instead of acknowledging the elephant in the room, Stevie simply nods her head as she finishes the rest of her sandwich. Once she's finished, she looks up at Rome and throws him another question. "There's still something I don't understand. If he's DEA, why is he going after me and my sister? Alex and I have nothing to do with The Organization. And I mean The Reapers obviously sell drugs, but so do all of the other syndicates in his jurisdiction. Why is he going after us specifically?"

"It has to be personal." I say, shaking my head. "He wouldn't go through so much trouble and do the horrific shit he's done if it wasn't. Maybe he's always hated The Reapers and now that he has power, he's doing everything he can to hurt them."

"Yeah, you're probably right." Stevie offers, slowly nodding her head. "So, where do we go from here?"

Rome takes a seat in one of the vacant armchairs next to me and grabs a sandwich of his own. "Dallas, Niko, and I are going to keep hunting. Letting Evanoff go free isn't an option. But you don't have to come with us. You're welcome to stay here and rest." He says, shifting his eyes between her and I. "I'm sure Violet

"I have to warn The Reapers." Stevie says, shaking her head. "They need to know who Dimitri really is and what he has planned."

"I think that's a good idea. The more people we have tracking him down, the better."

Stevie's brow furrows. "Wait, why didn't you guys just tell them from the beginning? Even if you didn't want to tell them about Alex just yet, they hate Dimitri. They'd be happy to have an excuse to wipe him out."

I knew this question was coming.

"They wanted to." I start, forcing the words out so The Mercenaries don't have to. "They knew where The Reapers stood with Dimitri's policies, but after surveying his interactions with you, it wasn't so clear to us how things would go anymore."

Stevie was friendly with him. Too friendly, and it was maddening watching her with him and knowing I couldn't do anything to warn her. "We wanted to tell The Reapers what was going on, but we couldn't risk the chance of you tipping Dimitri off."

Stevie slowly nods before turning her head towards the fire again. She visibly swallows as she tries to blink back the tears welling in her eyes. "I get it. That makes sense." She says, her voice slightly thick with emotion. "So, what happens next?"

I walk over to her and pull her in for a tight hug. *This isn't her fault. None of this is. Neither one of us could've predicted how this played out.* "You and I will stay here while The Mercenaries continue to hunt him. And when you're ready, I'll take you to go see The Reapers so you can tell them what's going on."

She stiffens in my hold. "Wait, you want me to go in person?" She asks, searching my eyes. "Why can't we just call them? It's faster and honestly, I'm probably the last person they want to see right now."

"We don't know what lines the DEA has tapped. We need someone to deliver the news in person. Someone they can trust. Out of the five of us, you're the only one that has a fighting chance at getting through to them."

NINE

Atlas

TWO WEEKS LATER

I KNOW what they're all thinking. Standing there watching the four of us like we're some kind of fucking anomaly. The question behind their eyes is so goddamn clear it's as if they etched it into their fucking corneas. *Where is she?*

Sorry assholes, hate to disappoint but even we don't have the answer to that million dollar question.

Grungy electronic music fills the air and as I take a swig of my whiskey, I swallow down the depressive thoughts right along with it. Between the warmth of the alcohol flowing in my chest and the deep vibrations of the bass, I'm feeling something other than nothingness, and that alone should be enough to get me through the night.

"So Atlas," Cyrus calls out, breaking me from my thoughts as he picks up his barely touched glass of cognac off of the coffee table in between us, "what's on the agenda for tonight?"

He casually swirls the amber liquid in slow circles as he awaits my answer, but when it becomes clear I don't have one for him, Tristan is quick to chime in.

"Is there a reason you w… wanted all of us here?" He asks, shifting his eyes pointedly between me and Cyrus and Ezra, who are seated on the other side of our lounge.

I glare at the empty space nestled between Ezra and Cyrus and grimace. *All of us… right.*

I suck my teeth and raise my glass of whiskey to my lips, biding my time while I think of an explanation.

Why did I want all of them here tonight? The answer is both a complicated and simple one. I'm fucking lonely. I miss them. I miss her. And as selfish as it is, I can't stand another night being alone with my thoughts.

I take a quick sip of my drink and as the liquid fire flows through me; I study all of their faces. At first glance, they seem to be holding up well, but the longer I stare, the more obvious it becomes that every single one of them is just like me. A ticking time bomb, seconds away from exploding.

Fuck. I can't tell them the truth. I'm supposed to be the stable one. The reliable one. The one that pulls them out when they're stuck in their own muddy thoughts. What kind of fucking leader would I be if I burdened them with my shit?

They're still expecting an answer, so instead of telling them the truth, I give them a much more palatable version of it. A version that makes it seem like their older brother still has his shit together and isn't just going through the motions with a gaping hole in the center of his chest.

"It's been a few weeks since the three of you have shown your faces here." I say casually as I level a stare at each of them. "Despite the changes in our lives, it's our obligation to keep up appearances."

"Speaking of appearances." Ezra says, standing up from his seat and smoothing out the non-existent wrinkles in his dark gray three-piece suit. "I'm due for one in the basement. Mind if I take off?"

I briefly hesitate before giving him a nod and after giving me a quick clap on the shoulder, he slips out of the lounge without another word.

I watch him leave and it's hard not to be concerned. I may be a wreck, but the way Ezra has been dealing with everything isn't much better. If he isn't out hunting for prey, he's in the basement, feeding his demons. It's a miracle he showered today, let alone threw on a fucking suit, but I suppose we're all excellent at playing our parts when we need to.

"Who's down there with him tonight?" Cyrus asks, making light conversation as he leans back into his seat.

"No idea." I say honestly, as I scratch at my beard. "It's hard to keep track of the revolving door of idiots that land on his bad side these days."

"I can't blame him." Tristan says with a scowl. "Lately, my patience has been wearing thin too. Speaking of, any word from The Mercenaries?"

"No, nothing knew." I say, shaking my head with a sigh. "Creed's team is just as frustrated as we are, but it's like the girl vanished. They've never hit a wall like this."

"Just call them off." Cyrus says with a shrug. "Tris and I have already taken over, anyway. It seems pointless to keep them on our payroll."

I figured this was coming. Ever since Stevie left, Tris and Cy have thrown themselves headfirst into the search for Alex. Tris is convinced that if he can just find her, everything will fall back into place. And fuck, I wish things were that simple. Cy is a bit more realistic. He knows the chances of finding her alive are minimal. He just doesn't have the heart to tell Tristan he's wasting his time.

"Yeah, I'll leave it up to you two." I reply, throwing back the last bit of liquid in my fifth glass of the night. "I'm fine with it either way."

Tristan and Cyrus exchange a look as I signal the server for another round, but I ignore the concern written all over their faces. I know what they're thinking. *This isn't me.* I don't relinquish control. I don't get drunk in the club, and I definitely don't leave things up in the air. But I'm starting to question if that's even the man I want to be anymore.

Ever since I can remember, I've always had this need for control. And until now, that control has never failed me. It kept us safe and kept a roof over our fucking heads and for me, that was enough. That is, until Stevie's sister went missing.

With a genuine threat hanging over our heads, my need for control took over. Instead of showing Stevie the empathy she deserved, I threw restraints on her without a second thought of how that would make her feel.

Her sister was fucking missing, but all I cared about was what I needed to do to make sure the same didn't happen to her. She deserved more than that and the truth is; I don't blame her for not coming back. *What kind of life could she even have with us?*

I sink deeper into the couch and stare at my brothers

as they start speaking to each other in hushed whispers. With the music pounding and my drunkenness finally kicking in, I let my head fall back and close my eyes. I'm fucking done thinking tonight.

"You should come home with us." Cyrus says, shaking my shoulder to rouse me awake. I don't know how long I was out, but if the furrow in his brow is any indication, it was long enough for them to be concerned. "Drowning your sorrows away here isn't helping anyone."

I shake my head and I let out a bitter laugh. That's what no one here seems to understand. *I'm doing all of this to help her.*

It's been weeks since Stevie vanished. Plenty of time for her to clear her head and try to make contact if she wanted to. We kept our distance because that's what she needed, but after the dust settled, she stayed gone. *That was her fucking choice.*

It may seem pointless now, but for once in my life, I'm going to let her decide. And if I have to be wasted 24/7 to stop myself from getting into my car and dragging her ass back home, then so fucking be it.

"Go home without me." I bite back, giving him a fake smile as I stare out into the crowd. "I'm staying. Besides, Ezra's going to need help with cleanup when he's done."

Alex's disappearance forced us to take a hard look at

the people we surround ourselves with. We still don't know who took her but, it's obvious, whoever it was, was close. So, for the interim, we're keeping our business, ours. Which means no cleanup crews and no unnecessary involvement with anyone who isn't family. At least until we find the mother fuckers responsible.

"Yeah." Cyrus bites back sarcastically. "I'm sure you'll be a big fucking help in the state you're in."

I narrow my eyes at Cyrus and it takes all the willpower I have to hold in the venomous shit I want to throw in his face. About how his messy track record with women and temper probably helped push her away, but I think better of it. We still don't know why she left and pointing the finger at each other is only going to make it worse.

Tristan stands up and forces himself in between us before turning to face me. "We're going to go get s… some air." He says, grabbing Cyrus by the lapel of his jacket and pulling him up off the couch. "But we aren't letting you s… stay here alone, asshole. So stop trying to get us to leave."

I can't help but smile to myself as I watch the two of them head towards the side door. He's right. I can be an asshole. Lately, more than usual. But he's a good kid. They both are. And I shouldn't be taking this shit out on either of them.

They don't show it, but I'm sure they're hurting too.

Stevie had a connection with all of us and fuck if that doesn't make things worse. Seeing any of my brothers in pain is hard, but having to watch all three of them go through this is a fucking nightmare, sober or not.

"Jack and Coke."

The sound of the server's voice breaks me out of my thoughts. She stands there for a few seconds, lingering just on the outskirts of my peripheral. She wants my attention, but I don't even bother acknowledging her presence. I have no patience for niceties tonight.

"All alone?" She asks, throwing her cleavage into my face as she leans over to set my drink down in front of me. "Where's that cute little girlfriend of yours?"

I resist the urge to laugh at her lack of subtlety and lean forward to pick up my glass as soon as she's clear. By now, I'm sure the entire club is painfully aware of Stevie's absence, but I'll bite. Anything is better than being alone with my thoughts.

"Don't know." I say, taking a slow sip as I stare out into the crowd. "And don't particularly care."

I smirk at the ease with which the lie slips from my lips. Maybe if I can convince her I don't care, I'll be able to convince myself.

"So you broke up?" She blurts, doing a shit job of disguising the excitement in her voice as her eyes widen. "I'm so sorry to hear."

Her act of sympathy is bullshit. She doesn't give a fuck about me any more than I give a fuck about her.

She's just asking what I'm sure everyone else in this place wants to know. *What happened to Stevie?*

I rest the glass on the edge of my lips and mull over her words with mild amusement. A fucking break up. God, if only the shit between Stevie and I were that simple. She wasn't just a girlfriend, or a casual fuck. *She was everything.*

The server mistakes the bitter expression on my face as an invitation and takes advantage of the opening. She sets her serving tray aside and moves behind me, bracing her hands on the edge of the couch.

"You poor thing." She coos, leaning over me in a not-so-subtle ploy to get closer. "You look so tense. Do you want to talk about it?"

I turn my head sharply, ready to tell her to back the fuck off, when her appearance stops me in my tracks. It's the server Stevie fought with. Chrissy? Kirsten? I should've recognized the voice as soon as she started speaking, but it's hard to focus on much of anything with this much alcohol in my system. She looks the same, only now, instead of her usual curly red ringlets, her hair is long, wavy, and dark, like Stevie's.

Seeing where my eyes linger, she instinctively strokes her hair. "I tried something different." She offers, with a hesitant grin. "Do you like it?"

I don't tell her the new color is the only reason I haven't kicked her out yet, but I don't need to. The choice was intentional, and it's written all over her face.

"Sure." I say, lowering my lids as the room starts to spin. There's a prominent slur to my word, but she doesn't seem phased by it. She's emboldened.

"Change is scary sometimes," she says, stepping around the couch to sit beside me, "but it can also be really good, if you're open to it."

It doesn't take a genius to figure out what she's suggesting.

I close my eyes and let my head lull back as she continues to drop more hints. I'm not interested in the slightest, but I'm the one who opened the conversation, so the least I can do is let her talk for a couple of minutes until she gets bored of me.

She will. Unless I give a shit about the person, I'm terrible at holding a conversation. Something about the monotony of small talk makes me want to gouge my fucking eyes out. It's all so vapid and shallow. If I'm going to talk to someone, I want it to mean something.

That's one of things I miss most about having Stevie around. Whenever I needed to talk, she was always there. Even before this whole thing really started. She was my best friend and now it feels like I have no one.

A hand grazes my thigh, and in an instant, I sober up. *What the fuck?*

I snap my eyes open and glare at the server with gritted teeth. I was wrapped up in my thoughts that I forgot she was here. What part of me blatantly fucking ignoring her made her think that shit was welcomed? *Fuck this*. She needs to leave. Now.

I grab her by the elbow and jerk her up off the couch, readying myself to give her the verbal lashing of a lifetime, but the second I catch a glimpse of the crowd surrounding us, I shake my head and have no fucking choice but to bite my tongue.

Fuck! Atlas you stupid asshole. Look what you did.

Nearly every single person in this building is watching our interaction play out. They all suspect that our queen walked away from her throne and by stupidly letting this woman get close to me, I've all but confirmed it.

Now the only way I can remedy this situation is to prove to them that losing Stevie hasn't changed us. That we're still the same vicious bastards any of them would be suicidal to cross with or without her at our side.

She isn't Stevie. Not by a long shot. But with everyone waiting for my reaction to her advances, that no longer fucking matters.

***

IF I THOUGHT for one second she'd have a problem with me using her, I'd be wrong. The minute I shot up from my seat and pulled her towards the back of the club, her eyes lit up and she gave me zero resistance. I hadn't even said another word to her, but she followed along giddily, smiling from ear to ear as I drunkenly yanked her through the crowd and up the stairs to my office.

She's malleable, so fucking malleable, and the old me, the one who existed before Stevie, would've enjoyed molding her to my whim.

Once we make it into my office, I take a seat behind my desk and the dizziness is nauseating. The world is fucking tilting, but I'm a glutton for fucking punishment, so I pour myself another drink, and let the space fill with uncomfortable silence.

"So..." She starts, glaring at me hungrily as she slowly catwalks towards my desk. "What should we do now?"

I flick my eyes up to her face and it's the first time I've been able to see her under normal light. She's attractive, in a conventional way, and most men would have no qualms about taking what she's so generously offering. But then again, most men haven't been ruined for anyone else, like I have.

"For the next 30 minutes? Nothing. Then you're free to go back downstairs."

She lets out a nervous laugh as her eyes dart around the room. "You're not serious."

"I am." I say flatly, slipping my phone out of my pocket and pulling up my emails. I can barely make out any of the words on the screen, but I need to get my point across. I'm not fucking touching her.

"It's a generous offer." I add, not even bothering to look up from my phone. "But I'm not interested."

She staggers back a little, as if my words have physically harmed her. "Why did you bring me up here?" She snaps, raising her voice in an attempt to cause a scene. The office is soundproof, so all she's doing is wasting energy.

I waste no time placating her and cut right to the chase. "Probably for the same reason that you wanted to be brought up here. For image. For ego. To show everyone else you could. You don't actually want to fuck me. You just want everyone to think that you did. The choice is yours. Stay and get what you really wanted or leave with nothing."

"I'll tell them you pussied out." She threatens, sticking her shaking chin out at me as her brows furrow in frustration. "That this was all a trick."

I tsk, shaking my head slowly as I slip a cigar from my pocket and methodically cut and light it. "You won't do anything." I deadpan, casting her a deathly glare. "Aside from the fact that disobeying me would be suicidal, you've signed an NDA. If so much as a whisper gets out about what really went on in here, I'll have my legal team so far up your ass you'll be vomiting men in blue suits. Not to mention I'll make sure that no one in the city ever hires you again. But if you're willing to throw your life away for a little ego trip, be my fucking guest."

"You know what?" She hisses, plopping herself into one of my leather seats. "You're a fucking asshole, Mr. Cole."

I smirk and let my eyes linger on the crowd pulsing below the glass floor. "So I've been told."

TEN

Ezra

"You know I never understood it. Why assholes like you live the way you do. You risk everything and make stupid decisions, all for a drug. For a fucking substance that's only real function is to poison your mind. It feeds you lies and yet, you worship that shit like it's your fucking god."

The man hanging in the center of my basement makes a wet gurgling sound as the ropes around his wrist twirl him in a slow circle. I'm not sure if it's a groan of agreement or one of pain, but I take it for what it is and continue on. I'm enjoying our little one-sided discussion. Besides, it's not like he's going anywhere else tonight.

"Take you, for instance." I say, taking a swig of my water bottle as I step up to him and kick a blank canvas underneath his body. "You're here because your addiction drove you to make some questionable choices. Choices that have real consequences. You should be angry at that fucking drug. After all, it's going to cost you everything. But I'm willing to bet the only thing running through your mind right now is how good it would feel to have one... last... hit."

At the premise of another hit, the man hanging in the center of the basement stirs to life. He forces one of his swollen eyes open and looks at me with a sense of longing that fucking depresses me.

"See what I mean?" I say, slapping the side of his swollen face as I toss my empty water bottle to the ground. "This isn't right."

"Stop taunting him, Ez." Stevie snaps, appearing behind the man's swaying body. *"You've punished him enough. Besides, you and I both know it isn't his addiction you're talking about."*

She moves closer and the fact that I can almost smell the sweet vanilla on her skin only confirms I'm losing my shit. She isn't real. *I know that.* But my imagination is a sadistic fuck and lately he's been throwing me this little five-foot-five curveball any chance he can.

Unlike the bloody motherfucker hanging in the center of the room, I can admit when I have a problem. But my drug of choice isn't any of that shit we sling to sustain our business. *It's her.*

Stevie is my addiction and trust me, I've tried everything I can to get clean. But she's the one bad habit I just can't break.

"Don't treat me like a problem." She says, reaching up to stroke my face. *"You and I... this thing we have... it's so much more than that."*

I jerk away from her hand and glare down at her. "Why the fuck do you keep doing this?"

It's the first time I've spoken to her since her appearances started, and it's obvious my question catches her off guard. Her eyes flare and she wraps her arms across her stomach as she mumbles out her reply.

"I wanted to check on you." She says softly. *"I'm worried about you, Ez."*

I clench my jaw and look away. *Right.* She may think she cares. *Hell,* she may even want to care, but things between us won't ever be the same. To her, I'll always be the man that killed her sister. That kind of betrayal never fades.

I stare at her for longer than I've allowed myself to in weeks, and feel myself visibly swallow. *Fuck, just looking at her like this is torture.*

Her long, dark hair frames the angles of her face in a chaotic halo of waves, creating a stark contrast to her fair golden skin. She's beautiful, but the storm behind her eyes fucking kills me. They have this wild look in them that tells me everything she does; she does viciously. She fights viciously; she fucks viciously, and she loves viciously. *Maybe that's why I can't quit her.*

Clearing my throat, I turn away and walk back towards my tray of implements in the corner of the room.

Fuck. I think, gritting my teeth as my fingers grip tightly onto the edges of the metal tray. *This has to stop.* If I keep playing into this, it's only going to fuel my obsession.

Letting out a sigh, I pick up the 9-inch bowie knife and grip the hilt tightly in my hand. I need a distraction and luckily for me, there's a perfect one still hanging in the middle of the room.

I turn to face him and feel the darkness inside of me takeover. *That's better.* I think, cracking my neck as I stride towards him. *It's time to get back to reality.*

"Hurting him won't make you feel better." She warns, moving to walk beside me. *"Nothing will."*

"Who says I want to feel better?" I snap, glaring at her as I sink my blade deep into the man's abdomen. He barely makes a sound as the blade punctures his gut and remains silent as long lines of blood drip down to the canvas below him.

"Maybe you're right." She whispers as she pivots

her head to stare at me. *"Maybe you don't. Is that why you lied about my sister?"*

Her accusation catches me off guard and I take a step back. *She can't know that.*

"I'm a figment of your imagination, remember?" She taunts, following my retreat. *"I know everything. Every dark little thought that goes on in that fucked up head of yours."*

For a second, I think about denying it, but there's no actual point. She isn't real, and all of this shit is merely an illusion. A literal manifestation of my own twisted mind.

She's right. I didn't kill her sister. Let me say that a-fucking-gain for good measure. I didn't kill her sister. *I lied.* But the way she looked at me that night. The desperate look in her eyes. That shit killed me, and it was the first time I could see what was really happening.

Stevie was losing herself. With each passing day, her need for vengeance was slowly driving her crazy. She almost killed Jessie and was seconds from going on a rampage to find answers. It was consuming her and I know from my own experience that once you welcome that darkness, it's almost impossible to find a way out. I couldn't let that happen to her. So I confessed to a crime that I didn't commit and gave her the closure she needed to move on. She already saw me as the villain in her story. What was another betrayal to add to the books?

"You should go." I bite out, shutting her down without bothering to confirm her accusation.

Her face falls and as she tightly clenches her fists, I see a sudden change in her demeanor.

"You know what your problem is?" She says, glaring at me with fire in her eyes. *"You treat me like you hate me, but deep down, I know the truth, Ezra Cole. You don't think you deserve me. That's why you keep pushing me away. You're on this mission to save my soul."*

I put on a sarcastic smirk as I look her up and down. "Don't flatter yourself, Angel. I don't give a shit about what happens to your soul."

"Angel." She scoffs, shaking her head at me. *"How fitting, considering you see yourself as a demon. You doomed us from the start. You put me on this impossible fucking pedestal and every time you see a hint of my darkness seep out, you think you're the one who put it there. Newsflash handsome, you aren't the only one with a past and as much as you don't want to acknowledge it, I was fucked up long before you came into the picture."*

It doesn't matter. None of this does. She isn't real. This thing in front of me is just a phantom, a reflection of my fucking guilt coming to haunt me.

"Leave." I say flatly, gesturing towards the door. "You've said your peace. Now I have work to do."

She cocks her jaw slightly and narrows her eyes at me. *"Oh, you do?"* She presses, eyeing me up and down.

"Last time I checked, work didn't include mutilating dead people."

My eyes flick over to the man hanging in the center of my basement, and the second I spot his motionless carotid artery, I curse.

Fuck. How did I miss that?

The man is dead alright and based on the amount of blood below his body; he has been for some time.

If I had a conscience, I'd feel bad for him. Then again, the bastard got exactly what was coming to him. Pro-tip if you're going to steal from a subset of The Russian Mafia, make sure you don't rip your face mask off until you're far out of sight of our cameras. The dumb fuck made it almost too easy for Tristan to find him. He took pictures of the drugs he stole and posted it all over social media.

The minute he chose to advertise his little come-up, he signed up for a one on one with me. No one touches what's ours and gets away with it. *No one.*

"So," Stevie taunts, standing beside me to lean her head on my shoulder, *"did hurting him make you feel better?"*

I don't dignify her question with a response. She and I both know the answer.

"I didn't think so. When are you going to wake up and realize that you'll never escape me? I'll haunt your every waking moment until you make this right. We

belong together. You're the only one who hasn't accepted it yet."

I've had enough. Of the taunting. Of the fucking delusions. I need to end this little warped fantasy once and for all.

"Do you know what happens to girls who fall for monsters?" I hiss, grabbing her by her jaw and shoving her hard against the wall. "I'm not talking about the fairy tale bullshit. I'm talking about real life. Do you know what happens to them?"

She shakes her head.

"They break." I snap, gripping her jaw so tightly I'm afraid it'll bruise. "Because no matter how much you try to change them, no matter how much you think you love me. A monster is still a monster. They can't love you back. All they'll ever do, all they can ever do, is destroy you."

Stevie tries to jerk out of my hold, but I just push her down harder. I raise my knife to her throat and as I press the sharp blade against her skin; I see a flicker of fear in her eyes.

That's more like it. I think, grinning down at her. *Remember who I am at my core, Angel. I'm not some broken boy you can fix. I'm a cold-blooded killer.*

"You want to hurt me?" She croaks, and I feel her chin tremble in my hand. *"You want to scar me like your past scarred you?"* Stevie shifts forward and before I can stop it, my knife sinks into her throat. *"I'd let you."* She

continues, moving closer and not even flinching when she forces the blade in deeper. *"I'd whisper sweet nothings in your ear while you sink your knife into me over and over again."*

She flicks her tongue against my earlobe and I visibly swallow, doing what I can to keep it together. *This isn't fucking real.*

"Something tells me you know that. That's why you've done everything in your power to push me away. But there's no denying our love. You hurt because you love me. You're just too fucking stubborn to admit it."

I jerk my knife away and shove her off of me, sending her crashing to the ground. I may be addicted to her, but what we have isn't love. Love is impossible for someone like me.

"I don't love." I say, shaking my head as I glare at the blood all over my hands. "It isn't in my fucking DNA."

"Is that so?" She asks, smirking at me as she pulls herself up from the floor. *"Then you should probably ask yourself, why is it that after all the deaths you've caused, and all the people you've hurt, I'm the only ghost that haunts you?"*

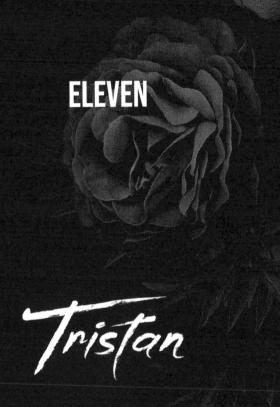

ELEVEN

Tristan

THE AIR OUT HERE IS FRIGID AS HELL. CYRUS AND I JUST stepped out into the alley and already I'm bouncing on my feet and rubbing my hands together to stay warm. Cy catches sight of me and laughs as he shakes his head.

"Should've kept your jacket on." He taunts, sinking his hands into his coat pocket for emphasis. "It's cold as hell tonight."

Thanks for the great observation, Sherlock.

I play with the idea of ripping his jacket off of him, just to teach him a fucking lesson, but think better of it. His mood has picked up and, as hilarious as it would be to see his reaction, I'm not going to be the one who sours it.

"It always is." I reply, bumping his shoulder with mine. "This city is like a f... fucking wind tunnel and this p... place is in the dead center."

We settle against the side of the building, doing what we can to shield ourselves from the icy breeze. Cyrus leans against the wall and as soon as the back of his head falls against the brick, he releases a long sigh. "I'm fucking sick of this place."

I laugh and shake my head at him. *I get it.* When we're at Hell's, it's all about putting up a front. About showing our power and keeping everyone beneath us in line. But it's hard to keep up the charade, especially when this is the last place any of us want to be right now.

We're fucking liars. Sitting there with our expensive whiskey and polished suits, pretending like we have all of our shit together, when in reality, we couldn't be more torn apart. We're devastated. Just going through the motions and barely holding our shit together. Atlas is the only one who seems mildly together, and that's just because he's better at hiding it than the rest of us.

Cy fetches a pack of cigarettes out of his coat pocket and slips a cigarette out for himself. He tilts the pack towards me in a gesture that's meant to be polite more than anything. He knows I don't smoke, but with every-thing going on in my head, I could use a distraction. I take him up on his offer and he only briefly hesitates before lighting the both of us up.

We stand there for a few moments, quietly enjoying the silence of the night as clouds of smoke swirl around us. The pounding house music playing inside is nothing more than a faint pulse out here and it feels good to hear myself think for once.

I slip my phone from my pocket and pull up the tracking app I installed on Stevie's phone. *Yes,* it's an invasion of privacy, and *no,* I don't feel bad about it. This app is the only thing stopping me from hunting her down, so she should be grateful I have it. I refresh her location and, just like it's shown for the last couple of weeks, she's still at Mel's. She never seems to leave, which would be uncharacteristic for anyone else. But after the fallout with Ez and everything going on with her sister, I'm sure the last thing she wants to do is go out into our city and chance a run-in with one of us.

"You're too quiet." Cy says, cutting into my thoughts as he rolls his head to level his eyes on me. "I know what you're thinking and you need to cut that shit now, before you do something stupid."

I give him a smirk and pull my cigarette to my lips, taking in a long drag as I think about my response. He's been this way since we were kids, always concerned about me and where my head is at. Most people see Cy as this playboy womanizer with a short fuse. But what they don't see, what he doesn't let them see, is that he is one of the most empathic fuckers I've ever met. He fights like hell for what he cares about and as much as he tries to hide it; he cares about a lot.

"Listen d… dad," I joke, glaring back at him, "we may have this weird twin-connection shit, but you aren't a f… fucking mind-reader. I'm not thinking anything." Not anything he needs to be worried about, at least.

Cyrus lets out a laugh as he lets out a cloud of smoke. "Fair enough." He offers with a nod. "I guess I just know what's been running through my head lately and assumed you were thinking the same."

"And what, d… dear brother, is that?"

"That we should go get her." He says, sobering up as he takes in another puff. "But that's a stupid idea."

I wasn't planning on doing anything yet, but I'd be lying if I said the thought hadn't crossed my mind. Instead of dropping the subject like he obviously wants to, I dig in further. "Why is it s… stupid?"

Cyrus lets out a sigh as he ashes his cigarette. "Because it isn't what she wants." He says simply, shrugging his shoulders as if he's already accepted defeat.

I release another lungful of smoke and glare at him. "How do you know what she wants?"

"I don't." He hesitates, clenching his jaw. "Not fully. But I know it's been weeks." He says, flicking his cigarette to the ground. "I know she knows where to find us. And I know no one is stopping her from coming back. She isn't here. That's all the proof I really need."

I take a deep breath as I mull over his words. "S... she just needs time to get over the s... shit with Ezra." I say, shaking my head. "She's been through a lot."

We still don't know what went down with those two. Once Ezra cooled off, Atlas tried to press him on the subject, but didn't get any definitive answers. Each of us tried to get him to talk, but after fighting with him for a few more days, we threw in the towel all together. Ez is a stubborn bastard and once he has his mind set on something, it's impossible to get him to change it.

"She hasn't made any contact." Cy says, snuffing out the flames of the discarded cigarette with the sole of his shoe. "If she wanted us, any of us, don't you think she would've said something by now?"

I run my hand over my face and take a second to think. *Is that really what's happening here?*

"Look, I get it." Cy adds, turning to face me. "I know what it's like to want something so bad you're willing to do anything to keep it. But trust me, forcing her to come back won't make anyone happy. She isn't ours anymore."

We stand there for a few moments in silence. Individually coming to terms with something neither of us wants to accept. As much as I hate to admit it, he's right. We can't force her to be with us. She wants her freedom, and after everything that's happened, the least we can do is give her that.

"Let's get back inside." Cy says, clapping me on my shoulder with a smile. "I'm sure Atlas is wondering what's taking us so long."

TWELVE

Tristan

Wʜᴇɴ ᴡᴇ ᴍᴀᴋᴇ ɪᴛ ʙᴀᴄᴋ ᴛᴏ ᴛʜᴇ ʟᴏᴜɴɢᴇ, Aᴛʟᴀs ɪs nowhere in sight. We take our seats anyway and wait it out for a few minutes, but when it's clear he isn't coming back, the two of us decide to go find him.

He may be the one that seems the most together, but that doesn't mean he's immune from doing reckless shit. Right now, we're all dangling close to the edge and all it could take is a little push for any of us to fall.

Cyrus and I cut through to the employee only entrance and make our way towards the back offices. More than likely, that's where he is and if he isn't there, at least we'll have a better vantage point to continue the search from.

We make it to his office and I'm just about to knock on the door when Cyrus stops me dead in my tracks.

"Wait." He whispers, leaning closer to the door. "Do you hear that?"

I follow his lead and easily pick up the muffled sound of someone talking. It's Atlas, and he sounds normal, if not a little buzzed, but these walls are supposed to be soundproof. I run my fingers against the seam of the door and when I notice it's slightly ajar; I curse under my breath.

Fucking sloppy, Atlas. What if one of our enemies had followed him back here to spy? Or worse, catch him with his fucking guard down. I'm half tempted to pull my gun on him just to show him how stupid that was. But when I hear a feminine voice pop into the conversation, my thoughts stutter to halt.

Cyrus turns to face me. "You don't think—"

"It has t... to be her." I reply, keeping my voice down.

"Why does he sound pissed?" He asks, as his brows draw together.

"She does too." I admit, picking up on the angry tone

in both of their voices. "We should give them privacy. Let them figure their shit out."

"No." Cyrus says, shaking his head. "You and I both know he's probably wasted by now. He's in no condition to talk to anyone. The last time we saw her, Ezra said something to drive her away, and we all had to deal with the consequences of his choice. I'm not taking a backseat this time around. I'm going in before At says something stupid. We all deserve the chance to say what we need to say to her."

Cyrus grabs the handle and forces the door open, nearly ripping the fucker off of its hinges. I think the time spent away from her made us all realize how much she means to us. How much, just having her in our home changes things.

The second Cyrus and I take in the scene before us, both of our faces fall.

"What the fuck is this?" I hear Cy shout among a stream of incomprehensible curses. I'm about to tell him to calm the fuck down when I realize he isn't the one screaming the string of words; *I am.*

It isn't like me to challenge Atlas. Then again, it isn't like me to care about what any of them do, but this doppelgänger version of our girl in his office is crossing several fucking lines.

I cut a scathing glance towards Atlas and feel the rage within me bubble up again. He's a grown man. He can do whatever the hell he wants, but this shit isn't okay.

"What the fuck are you still doing here?" Cy snaps, shifting his eyes to the carbon copy. "Get the fuck out. Now."

The woman bolts, nearly colliding with the two of us as she makes a beeline for the door. She's barely able to hold it together as she jerks the straps of her dress up and everything about this is fucking laughable. *What the hell was he thinking?*

"Sit down." Atlas snaps, making the woman freeze in her place. "We aren't finished here."

The woman turns around and tucks herself into the corner of the room, trying to make herself look as small as possible. It's a defense mechanism and a smart one, but it doesn't change the fact that she's still here.

"We have private matters to discuss." Cyrus snaps, tightly clenching his fists. "Send her away. Now."

It's obvious Cy's just as angry as I am. We've both looked up to Atlas our entire lives. He's supposed to be the smart one. The one that makes all the right decisions. But I think watching this shit play out is making us realize that maybe our big brother isn't so perfect after all.

"Say what you need to say." Atlas says, leaning back in his chair as he grabs a bottle and tops off his glass of whiskey. "Her NDA is bulletproof, and we've already discussed the ramifications she'll face if she decides to talk."

"This is low." I say, shaking my head. "And it isn't like you at all."

"Don't do that." Atlas snaps. "Don't tell me who I'm supposed to be. I know who the fuck I am. I'm the go to and I'm the only one in this family who's willing to do what it takes to keep us afloat."

"Let me guess." Cyrus adds, as his eyes shift between Atlas and the girl. "Fucking her was essential for the business."

Atlas scoffs as he swirls the whiskey in his glass. "Not that it's any of your fucking concern, but I didn't fuck her," he says, taking a long sip of his drink, "and I wasn't planning on it. I was simply doing what needed to be done. Something neither of you would know anything about."

He finishes his drink and stands up from behind his desk to walk towards us. "It must be so easy to navigate your fucking life when the only person you ever need to think about is yourself. I mean, Tris," he says, looking at me, "when things get rough you can just slink back behind your computer screen and no questions you. And Cy," he says, centering his focus on my twin, "isn't ironic that you're judging me for this when you used to fuck anything that smiled your way?"

"That was before." Cyrus hisses through gritted teeth.

Atlas scoffs. "Before what?" He asks, cocking his

head. "Before we tainted someone? Before we ruined her fucking life and selfishly dragged her into our world? Have either of you even thought about her in any of this? What would she gain by being with us? Huh? A life filled with danger and an early grave? Some fucking life, right? You both need to accept that she's better off without us and move the fuck on."

Cyrus gets quiet, and it's clear that everything Atlas is saying is getting to him.

"It wasn't like that." I say, trying to talk sense into both of them.

"It was always like that." Atlas retorts, with a sad smile. "And I, for one, am happy she got out of this shit. She's too good for us. *All of us.*" He says, glaring at me. "And it's time we accept that."

"You're so f... full of shit." I say, tilting my chin up. "You aren't happy. Look at you. You're d... drunk. You haven't shaved in weeks. Your s... suit is fucking wrinkled. And you may act like you're fine, but everyone can s... see how fucked up you are. You miss her."

Atlas clenches his jaw as he lets out an exasperated sigh. "Missing her and holding my fucking breath for her are two separate things, baby brother. She isn't coming back."

"You're lying to yourself." I hiss, shaking my head. "And you entertaining this f... fucking imposter," I point out, glaring at the woman that still hasn't taken the fucking hint, "proves it."

Stevie isn't some innocent girl we tainted for fun. She belongs with us and she's so much stronger than any of us give her credit for. She'll stop at nothing to protect the people she cares about and she loves the fuck out of us. She's one of us, and just like I wouldn't ever give up on any of my brothers, I'm not giving up on her.

Fuck this. It's obvious the both of them are too wrapped up in their own guilt to see the truth. Trying to talk sense into them is a waste of my time. I'm about to storm off when Atlas says something that catches me off guard.

"You're right." He says, letting out a heavy sigh as he runs a hand through his dark hair. "Bringing her up here was a mistake and I've been making way too fucking many of them lately."

He glares at the woman. "In case you weren't sure, this is your cue to get the fuck out."

Atlas returns to his seat behind his desk and refills his glass. There's a deep tiredness in his eyes that I didn't notice before. This has been just as hard on him as it's been on any of us. "Also, change your hair back to its original color or consider yourself fired."

"What?" The woman snaps back, shooting up from her seat. "That isn't fair. You can't force me to do that." She says, cutting her eyes over to me and Cyrus. "He can't make me do that."

"Actually," Cyrus retorts, cocking his head at her with a callous smirk, "he can. As part of your terms of employment, any physical changes to your image must be approved through management first. We are well within our rights to fire you. Be grateful Atlas decided to give you a second fucking chance, because if it were up to me, I'd throw your ass out without another thought."

"Leave," I add, glaring at her, "before we have s... security drag you out."

She heads for the door in a fit of rage, huffing and puffing as she stomps away. It's clear she's doing it to garner attention, but none of us bother to give her a second glance. She may be a replica of the only woman that ever made us give a fuck, but that doesn't mean we need to give a fuck about her. She doesn't come close to Stevie. *No one does.*

THIRTEEN

"Stop fidgeting." Alex says, casting me a side-eyed glance as she takes a sharp right turn. "You're making me nervous. Besides, I don't know what you're so worried about. Everything is going to be fine."

That's easy for her to say. She doesn't know them like I do.

I smooth out the wrinkles in the jade slip dress Alex

let me borrow and take a deep breath to ease some of my nerves.

This visit is long overdue. I should've gone to see them the minute they told me what was happening, but I just kept putting it off. First, I wanted to wait until the swelling was gone. Then it was until the bruises faded. But now? Now it's been two weeks and I'm all out of excuses.

I'm scared to see them.

I've been living with this idealistic version of them in my head for so long, I've grown used to it. A version of them that still cares for me and misses me just as much as I miss them.

But what if I'm wrong?

What if they've moved on? What if they've realized their life is much easier without me?

If that's the case, I wouldn't even blame them. They warned me about Dimitri. They told me to stay far away from him and what did I do? I went behind their backs and befriended that bastard.

Feeling the need to focus on something other than everything I don't want to think about, I flip open the passenger mirror and reapply concealer over the scar on my cheek. Concentrating on the task helps to steady my shaking hands for a moment, but as soon as I'm done, my heart rate kicks up again.

I can't do this. How the hell am I going to face them?

"They need to know what's going on." Alex says,

giving me a smile as she reaches over and links her hand with mine. "And they're going to be happy to see you."

Maybe.

I know I miss them. I know I'm sorry. And I know they deserve to know what happened. But my fear is getting in the way.

Alex pulls into a familiar alleyway and my stomach drops a few notches. I knew where we were going, but it feels so different to be this close. To know my reunion with Atlas, Ezra, Cyrus, and Tristan is just moments away.

She parks her car near the front of the building and when I don't see anyone lingering by the entrance, I let out a little sigh of relief. I don't think I could stomach a crowd of people watching me come back into the club after so long.

I step out of the car and before we part ways, Alex tosses me something through her window. "Keep it on you." She orders, holding my gaze after I catch it. "Just in case."

I toy with the burner phone she tossed me and give her a slow nod.

I still can't get over how different she is. She's harder now. Stronger. Nothing like the kid I left behind. It's not necessarily a bad thing, it's just… different, and it's something I'm still trying to get used to.

I hold her gaze for a little bit longer. "I'm not going

to need this, you know." I say, dangling the phone in the air. "I'm coming back tonight."

She flashes me a knowing smile. "Well, if you decide not to come back tonight, I won't blame you." She says, shaking her head. "Don't worry about me. Now that The Reapers are getting looped in, the guys are probably just going to want me to lie low at the house until this whole thing is taken care of. Do what you need to do to make things right with them, just don't disappear on me again."

In the weeks we've been together, she hasn't told me much about what happened to her while we were separated, but from the bits and pieces I've gathered, life hasn't been easy for her.

I never wanted that for Alex. In fact, I did everything I could to prevent it. But I'm proud of the person she is now, even if I had little to do with it.

After parting ways, I slip the burner phone into one of my boots and make my way to the front door. Once inside, I navigate through the crowd with my chin down and my long dark waves obscuring most of my face. The last thing I need to do right now is bring any attention to myself.

Dimitri thinks I'm dead, so I doubt he has spies in here looking for me, but I can never be too careful. I know better than to put anything past that monster.

I slip into the back hallway without anyone noticing and as I trek through the familiar dark corridor that leads up to the back staircase, nostalgia hits me hard. *It feels so much like the first night I came here. The first night I was introduced to their world.*

My boots feel like they're filled with lead as I trudge up the staircase and the irony of how this must look isn't lost on me. There's no one forcing me to go up. No gun digging into my back, and yet here I am, acting like I'm being marched to my own fucking grave.

Once I reach Atlas' office, I take a deep breath, mentally preparing myself for what comes next. *You can do this.* I think to myself. *They deserve to know.*

All I have to do is knock on that door and spit the words out. *Easy.* As long as I don't choke on them first.

I raise my fist and do everything I can to steel my nerves as I go to knock, but before my knuckles can even contact the wood, the door swings open and out walks a familiar face.

I fixate on the woman, too surprised by what I'm seeing to think better of it. *It's the cocktail server.* The same one that all but threw herself at Atlas the last time I was here.

I study her from head to toe. Analyzing every noticeable change from her freshly dyed dark hair, to the black mini dress she's spilling out of that bears a striking resemblance to one of my own. The more I stare, the more repulsed I feel. Either I'm delusional or she's transformed herself into some warped fun-house mirror version of me. *What the hell is this?*

As if she can read my mind, the clone raises her hand to her mouth and wipes the corner of her lips in such a crude way that there's no need for me to try to figure out what she was doing in there.

It's fine. I remind myself. *He's an adult and a single one at that, and he can do whatever the hell he wants.*

I look behind her, and even though I'm trying like hell not to care, what I find stabs me deep in the pit of my stomach. *Atlas isn't alone.* Cyrus and Tristan are flanking his sides and all three of them look particularly out of sorts.

I want to be angry. I want to channel this pain I feel into rage and snap at all of them. But that isn't fair. I'm the one that left them and I've been MIA for almost a month. They have every reason to try to move on with their lives and I can't stake a claim on something I let go. I just have to face the reality of the situation. They aren't mine anymore.

I give the cocktail server a blank stare and as she moves past me; she lets one last dig slip from her lips. "Don't look so surprised." She taunts, smirking at me. "I told you he'd want to explore other options."

I cling to my detached expression like a shield of armor and stand there silently as she slinks away.

This shouldn't hurt. I think to myself as I clench my jaw and shove the sadness trying to surface back down. *You're the one who left them, and this shouldn't hurt.* I think again, sinking my nails into my tightly clenched palms to try to distract myself.

But it does. It hurts like hell.

The door softly closes shut and I wait for a few minutes to pass before attempting to knock again. They don't need to know what I saw, it'll just make things more complicated.

"Come in." Atlas calls out and for a moment I'm surprised at how good it feels to hear his voice. Even in his businessy, professional tone, it's comforting in a way I didn't expect.

I glide the door open and stand in the doorway with my arms crossed over my chest. "Hey." I say, giving them all a little smile as I take a quick survey of the room. "I hope I'm not interrupting."

All three of them stare at me with mixed expressions and wide eyes. It's the first time I've ever seen them look so surprised, and if the circumstances were different, it would almost be funny.

Cyrus is the first to snap out of it. He shoots up from his seat and his long legs swallow the distance between us in a matter of seconds. Before I even have time to react, he lifts me up in his arms and pulls me in for a tight hug.

He coils his arms around me and hoists my legs around his waist, sinking his face deep into the crook of my neck. He smells like the end of summer, all citrusy and warm and bittersweet.

"God, I've missed you, P." He confesses, breathing the words into my neck. *I missed you too,* I want to say, but I hold myself back. *I can't say things like that to them anymore.*

He's held me before, but something about the way he's holding me now feels different. More protective. Like as long as I'm in his arms, nothing bad will ever happen to me.

God, I wish that were true.

All I want to do is soak up this moment, but this feeling is just part of a fantasy. Some fairy tale illusion I used to think I could have. It isn't real. None of this is. In the real world, bad shit happens and in the real world, I lost them.

I pull away from Cyrus and climb out of his hold. He releases me without too much resistance, but when he notices the sadness in my eyes, he grabs a hold of my elbow and pulls me back towards him.

"You okay?" He asks, peering into my eyes as he hooks a finger under my chin and tilts my head up. The sincerity I see in his eyes pulls me in and the impulse to melt into his touch is almost immediate.

What am I doing? I think, chastising myself. I know what I just walked in on and yet here I am, letting my feelings for them get the best of me. I need to get it together. *Now.* Before I lose sight of what's important.

"I'm fine." I reply, pulling myself out of his hold. Cy staggers back a little as if the rejection physically harms him, but in an instant he recovers, smoothing his features and taking a few steps back as if it never happened.

It doesn't surprise me. The Cole brothers have a knack for hiding their feelings, especially when it comes to me. It's time for me to do the same.

"Do you guys have a minute?" I ask, forcing myself to get straight to the point. "There's something I need to talk to you about."

"What's wrong?" Atlas asks, furrowing his brow as he moves from behind his desk and walks up to me. "Is something going on? Are you in some kind of trouble?"

"No." I say, shaking my head. "No, it's nothing like that."

"What is it?" Tristan asks, stepping forward as he searches my eyes. "Whatever it is, we can f… figure it out. You're home. That's all that m… matters."

I take in a sharp inhale and worry my lip. I'm trying my best to get over them, but when they say things like that, it pulls me right back in. "I'm not staying." I force out, looking away to hang on to the little composure I have left.

"What are you talking about?" Atlas asks as a look of genuine confusion crosses his face. "Of course you're staying."

"I'm—" I stammer, trying to remember the words I practiced in the drive over. I thought I could do this, but it's so much harder than I ever imagined it would be. The thought of telling them the truth about what happened to me makes me physically sick.

Despite the fact that they didn't come for me.

Despite the fact that they were here with someone else.

I don't want to hurt them. And regardless of where we stand now, I know them well enough to know that finding out what Dimitri did to me, will hurt them.

Heat spreads up my neck as their eyes bore into me and all I want to do is bury myself in the ground. *This was a mistake.* I should've just let The Mercenaries be the ones to deliver the news.

Atlas searches my eyes as he watches a kaleidoscope of emotions flicker across my face. "Kitten." He says, placing his calming hand on my shoulders. "What the hell is going on?"

FOURTEEN

Stevie

I FUCKED UP. I WANTED TO CHOOSE MY WORDS carefully. To break it to them in the simplest and easiest terms I could. But as soon as I opened my mouth, it was like I couldn't hold all of it in anymore and the words just started pouring out.

I told them *everything*. About Dimitri and how he set us all up. About The Mercenaries and their role in protecting Alex and ultimately saving me. I even told them about what happened the first night I met Dimitri and the subsequent texts he sent me after that.

I don't know what came over me. And I still don't know what they're thinking. I stopped talking a few minutes ago, but the three of them have yet to say a word.

Atlas looks at me like he's in mourning. He keeps running his hands over his beard and staring at me like I'm some lost soul he was too late to save. And because he's who he is, I'm sure he's blaming himself for this.

Cyrus is sitting on the edge of Atlas' desk, glaring at me like I make him uncomfortable. He keeps clenching and unclenching his jaw, as if the mere sight of me is agony. I hate that hurting him seems to be the only thing he can rely on me for.

Tristan is standing behind his brothers, studying me with that quiet intelligence I've always admired about him. Out of the three of them, he's the only one I can't get a read on. There's some anger there, but I can see questions lingering behind his eyes.

"Did anything else happen?" Atlas asks abruptly as his eyes zero in on me. "Anything else you're not telling us?"

I glance between the three of them. "No." I say, shaking my head as I quickly scour through my confession. "I'm pretty sure that's everything."

"Did they hurt you?" Tristan asks, narrowing his eyes at me.

"What?" I ask numbly, blinking at him slowly before breaking eye contact to look down at my hands. I start picking at my nonexistent calluses as my thoughts race.

Fuck. I didn't even realize I left that part out. The torture was the most horrific part of the entire ordeal. Maybe my mind just blocked it out. It was worse than the fire. Worse than when he dragged me out of Melanie's. But what good is it going to do if I tell them I was tortured? They're already going to go after Dimitri regardless, and finding out *why* he tortured me will only end up hurting them. I'm not going to tell them. They've already had enough hurt from me to last a lifetime.

"Besides the fire." Cyrus adds, grabbing my attention as he forces himself up from the desk. "Did he or his men do anything else to you?"

I swallow and stare at the three of them, mildly thrown off by their response. I expected them to be more mad at me. To accept my mistakes for what they were and then throw me out on my ass without an ounce of remorse. It would've hurt like hell, but I could've survived it.

But this. This is something I didn't see coming. The three of them are trying, and I mean, *really* trying, to understand what I've been through. It's obvious they don't like the choices I made, but they haven't placed any of the blame on me. I should be grateful, but somehow, their concern for me is only making this harder.

Atlas moves out from behind his desk and takes a

seat in the vacant chair beside me. "Look," He says, reaching over to link his fingers with mine. His touch is warm yet solid, and all I want to do is climb into his lap and pretend that everything's okay. That everything that happened was all a bad dream. "Whatever happened to you changes nothing."

"We just need to know." Tristan adds, rounding the desk to perch beside me.

I close my eyes and slowly shake my head.

"What is it?" Cyrus asks, kneeling in front of me as he cups my chin and forces my head up.

"No." I lie, my voice barely above a whisper. "Nothing like that. Just the fire."

I want to be honest with them, but right now, their safety comes first. If they find out I was tortured, it'll add even more emotion to this already volatile situation and they could end up getting themselves hurt. I'll tell them the full truth. Soon. But not now. I've already spilled enough truths tonight.

Satisfied with my answer, the guys retreat back to their seats and, after a few moments of uncomfortable silence, I speak up.

"I should get going." I say, standing up from my seat. "Alex is outside waiting for me."

A storm of emotions flashes across their faces. From shock to sadness to anger. I want to look away, but it's so raw that it almost feels cowardly to shy away from them.

"Why are you leaving so soon?" Cyrus asks, cocking his head as he narrows his eyes at me.

"Well, we're done here." I say, shifting my eyes between the three of them. "I told you guys everything and there's really nothing left to say—"

"Stay with us." Atlas says, holding my gaze for a few seconds. "At least, until the Dimitri problem is taken care of. All of your things are still at the house. It doesn't make sense for you to stay anywhere else."

Should I? Alex said it would be fine if I stayed with them and it would be nice to wear clothes that fit me for a change. *Alright.* I can handle a few days with The Reapers. I mean a month ago, I was ready to spend a life-time with them.

"Okay." I say, nodding my head. "I can do that. Let me just make a call first."

FIFTEEN

Stevie

FUCK, WHY THE HELL DID I AGREE TO COME BACK HERE?

As soon as Tristan pulled up the driveway, the tightening in my chest started. And now that I'm hovering just outside of my old bedroom, it literally feels like I'm going to pass out.

There's too much history. Too many emotions, and just being under the same roof with them feels impossible. I headed straight upstairs for a reason, but even this hallway is tainted. It smells like a heady mixture of them. I'm trying my best to get over my feelings for them, but this place is like a time capsule of our relationship. Forever reminding me of everything I lost.

I lean against the wall and stare up at the ceiling. Almost as if to remind myself that, despite how it feels, the world isn't actually caving in on me.

I can do this. They've moved on with their lives and I need to do the same. *This'll be good for me.*

I close my eyes and search my mind, scouring through every inch until I can find it. The tiny little box that once stored all of my emotions. I never thought I'd need it again, but right now everything feels so overwhelming and I'm grateful as hell I still have it.

I take my time plucking each volatile emotion from my brain and placing them into my tiny box one at a time. I do this over and over again until I'm left with nothing. I know that concealing my feelings for them isn't an actual solution, but it's the only way I'll be able to get through the rest of my time here. Things between us will never be the same and I have no one but myself to blame for that.

"What the fuck are you doing here?"

The venom behind the question feels so intense that for a second, I convince myself there's no way it's directed at me.

I open my eyes and when I take in the man staring

back at me; I realize, with quiet certainty, that I'm exactly who it's intended for.

Ezra stands there glaring at me with so much disdain in his eyes it makes me uncomfortable. My stomach twists in a tight knot and it's hard for me to pull in anything more than quick shallow breaths.

"Haven't you done enough?" He asks, inching closer to me with an almost feral look in his eyes. He smells just like I remembered. Lavender mixed with a heady dose of danger. Against my better judgment, I breathe him in, and am instantly brought back to the memories we've made together, both good and bad.

"Answer me." He snaps, ripping me away from my thoughts. "I thought I told you to disappear. Why the fuck are you here?"

Shit.

I look up at him, and I don't even know how to begin answering his question. I'm here because I'm forced to be. I'm here because I want to be. I'm here because leaving you and your brothers was the hardest thing I've ever had to do.

He's angry. I can see it in the slight twitch of his hands and the way his chest is rising and falling. I don't waste any more time mulling over the right thing to say. I just tell him what I've been wanting to tell him ever since Dimitri revealed what he did to Alex.

"I'm so sorry, Ezra." I confess, stepping towards him.

"I'm sorry for hurting you. For pushing you to hurt me. I'm just really fucking sorry."

I place my hand on his cheek and the way his body stiffens under my touch nearly brings back some of the painful emotions I just locked down. I search his eyes, hoping to see something, anything, to show me he believes me, that he can feel just how sorry I am. But there's no sign of understanding in his eyes. Only anger.

"You're good." He offers as a bitter smile forms on his lips. "For a second, I almost believed you. That was the realest you've ever felt."

What the hell is he talking about? "I've always been real with you, Ez."

He laughs, shaking his head before glaring at me again. "That's not what I'm talking about, and you know it."

"What?" I ask, cocking my head in confusion. "What are you talking about?" This conversation has taken a swift turn and I'm completely lost.

Ezra glares at me, working the muscles in his jaw as he slowly cracks his neck. I take a step back, not liking where any of this is going, and at the sight of my retreat, something inside of him snaps.

He rushes towards me with lightning fast reflexes and grabs hold of my throat. I pound on his arm in a panic, but that only seems to amplify his fury. He shoves me against the wall behind us so hard that my head bounces against it on impact.

I'm terrified.

Ezra gets in my face, pressing his nose against mine as he painfully tightens his grip on my throat. "Don't act stupid." He hisses. "You know exactly what the fuck you're doing."

I fervently shake my head as I try to pry his tight fingers off of my throat, but it's no use. He has a death grip on me and my muscles are growing weaker by the second. I want to ask him why, but a part of me already knows the answer. I hurt him.

Panic sinks into every inch of my body, paralyzing me. He's going to kill me. *I don't want to die.* Not here and definitely not like this.

"You're poisonous, Angel." He says, with a sad smile as he presses a slow kiss to my cheek. "I'll always crave you, but I have to stop you before you destroy me."

I still, at his words. *He's right.* I am poisonous. I destroy everything I care about. First Alex, then Melanie, and now... coming back here after all of this time is destroying them.

I have no right to expect anything from them. I can try to tell myself I didn't have a choice, but there's always a choice. I just consistently make the wrong ones.

A silent tear streams down my cheek as I feel the fight within me die. Maybe this is for the best. At least if I die, I won't be able to hurt the people I care about most anymore.

"Come on, Angel." Ezra pleads as he slowly shakes

his head. "Don't cry. You're making this harder than it needs to be."

I close my eyes, shielding myself from the sadness I see in his. My lungs are on fire and every inch of my body is screaming in pain. I can't hear anything around us, except for the sound of my heart pounding in my chest, but I don't feel sorry for myself. *I can't.*

I deserve this. *I deserve all of this.*

SIXTEEN

Ezra

As I watch the life drain from her eyes, a strange feeling settles over me. At first, it barely registers, like a faint whisper in the back of my mind, telling me that something is wrong. But in an instant, it multiplies, intensifying until it's grating against every bone in my fucking body.

Stop. Stop. STOP!

I release her throat with a curse and quickly back off.

What the fuck was that?

Stevie's ghost sinks to the ground and gasps for air in between bouts of violent coughs. She's a talented actress, I'll give her that. The bright red bruises forming around her neck are a nice touch and if I didn't know any better, I'd think I really did some damage.

"Leave." I say flatly, keeping my voice cold and detached. I've played into her antics too much as it is. Anymore of this talking with a ghost shit and I'll need to be institutionalized.

She gets to her feet, but instead of walking away like she knows she should, she staggers towards me. "Do you really hate me that much?" She asks, peering up at me with her bloodshot eyes.

I clench my jaw and avert my eyes. "That doesn't fucking matter."

"It does, Ez." She whispers, nodding her head softly as she blinks back the tears welling in her eyes. "It matters to me."

I snap my head towards her and say the first thing that comes to mind. "I hate what you've turned me into. What you've turned us all into. You had no fucking right to come into our lives and wreck us the way you did." The words aren't just for this phantom, but I still feel them all the same. I hate what she did to us.

"Then finish it." She insists, reaching for my hand and wrapping it firmly around her throat. "If that's what you really want, I won't stop you." She says the words with so much conviction that for a moment, I'm not sure what to do.

If I go through with this, there's a good chance I'll lose the only traces of Stevie I have left. *Is that something I even want?* I'm not sure, but anything is better than continuing to be driven into madness by the one thing I can't have.

I squeeze her throat tighter, letting my fingers sink deeper into her warm, soft flesh. She closes her eyes, and as her head falls back, a trace of a smile touches her lips.

God, she's so beautiful. It's sick how badly I still want her, even in this nonexistent form, even when all she's ever done is fucked with my head. I'm still as addicted to her as I was the first night we met. I thought I could shake this, but I don't think my craving for her will ever go away.

I take in everything. Her trembling full lips. The influx of emotion on her face. And the feeling of her pulse drumming against my fingertips.

Normally she's muted, like she's just remnants of a girl I once knew. But my mind is amplifying her to a new level. I can almost taste the sweet vanilla & nectar on her skin.

I fixate on her throat and squeeze a little tighter, feeling the muscles in her neck strain against the pressure. I look up at her face and try to capture everything one last time before she's gone. Every line, every scar, and every freckle. I hate that I'm going to miss her. I should fucking hate her. But I can't.

My eyes linger on a scar that starts a centimeter above the hollow of her cheek and goes up, fading just before it approaches the corner of her eye. My body goes cold.

I've memorized every mark on this woman's body. Every minute detail, and I can guarantee I've never seen this fucking scar before. I've replayed the night she left over and over again in my head, and I'm positive it wasn't there that night. *So where the fuck did it come from?*

I release her throat a fraction and as her lungs pull in large gasps of air, the color returns to her face. *Everything about her is real, too fucking real.*

Her eyes fly open and as she stares at me with a mixture of confusion and shock, the dots finally connect.

No. I think, clenching my jaw as I stare back at her. *It can't be.*

In an instant, our connection is severed and I'm pummeled across the hallway by a wall of brute force strength. My back slams into the opposing wall with a loud crack and as I try to right myself, it takes a few seconds for me to catch up to what's just happened.

"What the fuck is wrong with you?" Cyrus snarls, shoving me back against the wall again as he gets into my face.

She can't be real. I think numbly as I slowly shake my head. *It's not possible.*

Cyrus continues to spew more shit my way, but all of his words fall on deaf ears. I'm concentrating on one thing and one thing only, *Stevie.* I look up and hold her gaze.

She is real, and I almost fucking killed her.

Tristan notices me staring and, like the overprotective asshole he is, he steps into action. "Don't f... fucking look at her." He snaps, moving in front of her to block my view. "Not until you explain what the f... fuck just happened."

Tension crackles in the air as neither Stevie nor I make a move to speak. I could try to explain myself, but I doubt either of them would believe me and I know she won't.

Stevie steps out from behind Tristan and tries to bring the focus back to her. "It's fine." She offers, waving them off as she takes a minute to catch her breath. "I'm fine. We were just talking."

The twins' reaction is immediate. "Talking, huh?" Cyrus asks, glaring at me, knowing full well that what she said is complete bullshit. "Is that what was happening?"

No. I think, clenching my jaw. *I almost fucking killed her.*

Instead of revealing my thoughts, I just give him a stiff nod and keep my mouth shut.

Tristan sneers at me as he narrows his eyes. "That doesn't look like t... talking." He says, pointing out the bright red marks around Stevie's neck.

Stevie instinctively wraps her hand over the marks and casts her eyes down. "It's nothing." She mumbles, shaking her head with a half-hearted smile. "It was an accident."

I glare at her. *Why the hell is she trying to sweep this under the rug?* I know it was an accident, but she doesn't. And while we're at it, what the fuck is she even doing here?

I look between Tristan and Cyrus and can see the cogs turning in their heads. My brothers are more of the shoot first, ask questions later type, and I can tell that both of them are raring for a reason to lay my ass out. They should. I'd do the same if any of them hurt her. The only reason they haven't is because she's covering for me. The question is, *why?*

I'm missing something. My brothers don't seem surprised to see her here, and Stevie's behavior isn't adding up. *What aren't they telling me?*

"What are you doing here?" I ask, leveling my eyes at her.

Tristan snaps his head towards me. "She hasn't t... told you?"

"Told me what?" I retort, shifting my gaze between her and my brothers.

"She's staying with us." Atlas calls out, stepping out

of his bedroom to join us in the hallway. "And whatever just happened." He says, giving each of us a hard look. "Is over now. Understand?"

We all give him a nod.

"Good. Now it's been a long night and I'd really like to get some sleep sometime before dawn. Ez, I know you're probably confused right now, but I'll fill you in on everything in the morning."

And on that note, the five of us slowly part ways. Atlas walks back into his room and the twins follow Stevie back to hers, leaving me alone with my thoughts in the hallway.

I still don't know what led her here, but at this point, I honestly don't care. All that matters is that she's back and this time around, there's no way in hell I'm letting her go without a fight.

SEVENTEEN

"ARE YOU HURT?"

Tristan asks, pulling his brows together in a scowl as he and Cyrus take a seat beside me on the bed. He gently grazes his thumb against the red marks on my neck before flicking his eyes back up to me. "They look like they hurt."

I tilt my chin down as I shake my head. "No." I say. "Honestly, I'm fine." And even if I wasn't, I wouldn't let them feel sorry for me. The worst of the choking happened the second time, and I literally forced him into it.

Cyrus locks eyes with me. "What the hell happened back there?"

I don't even really know myself. I think we both just got swept up in the moment. Ezra wanted to punish me for hurting him and I wanted to be punished for the same reason. But I don't think he meant for any of that to happen. It was like he was in a trance and once he snapped out of it, the regret on his face was immediate. "It's nothing for you two to concern yourselves with." I say, trying to make light of the situation. "Things between Ez and I are... complicated."

They both release a heavy sigh. "He's our brother, but that d... doesn't mean we're okay with him hurting you." Tris says, shaking his head.

"You're right." I say, nodding my head. "And once he cools down, I promise I'll have a talk with him about it and we'll explain everything. But tonight, can you just trust me when I say that it was all just a big misunderstanding?"

"Of course." Cyrus says, giving me a nod as he moistens his lips. "But if it happens again, next time we won't be as understanding."

It won't. I'm sure of it.

"I get it." I say, nodding my head. "But for tonight,

can we just get into bed and forget about what just happened?"

Both of their heads snap towards me and the unmistakable look of heated desire crosses their faces.

Wow. I didn't even know that was something they'd be open to, but now that it's in my head, it won't go away.

"Our own… beds." I add hastily, wincing a little at how much more awkward I made it.

Cyrus smirks as he shakes his head at me. "Come on, Tris." He says, patting his brother's shoulder as he stands up to his full height. "Let's let her get some sleep."

Tristan follows his lead, trailing after him as he heads for the door. "If you need anything," Tris says, holding my gaze. "We're s… sleeping right outside your door tonight. Just in case."

I shake my head. "You guys don't have to do that."

"We want to." Cyrus adds, lingering by the door. "You should always feel safe with us, P."

"Thanks." I say, flashing them a grin as they shut the lights off and quietly shut the door behind them.

It takes some time, but when I finally fall asleep, I rest easy knowing that if anyone tries to hurt me, they'll have to make it through the two tattooed walls of muscle stacked behind my door.

———————

THE NEXT MORNING, I wake up starving. I was too nervous to eat the day before, but now that my nerves have settled, the hunger is starting to catch up with me.

I take a quick shower and slip into the only clean clothes I have, a pair of black yoga pants, a cream cropped top that's way too short on me and my favorite furry ice-blue house slippers that I forgot to take with me to Mel's.

I walk out of my room and before I even take two steps, one of my slippers gets caught on the pile of blankets laying just outside my door and I nearly fall face first to the ground. Luckily, I catch myself, but I still silently curse at the obvious culprits.

Fucking, Tristan and Cyrus.

I want to be mad at them for leaving a freaking death trap in front of my door, but I can't find any real reason to be upset. I'm still not over the fact that they guarded my room all night. It was a really sweet gesture and something I definitely don't deserve.

I walk down the hallway and the second I pick up the scent of garlic and onions wafting up the stairs, my stomach grumbles.

I make my way towards the kitchen and when I find

all four of them cooking breakfast; I find myself at a loss for words.

"Morning." Cy says, smirking at me as he snatches a piece of bacon from one of the platters. "Nice outfit."

I tug at my shirt to cover up the slice of underboob hanging out and he pouts. "I haven't done laundry," I shrug. "And for some strange reason, I totally forgot to pack a bag."

"Funny." He notes with a laugh. "Take a seat. Breakfast is almost ready."

"You guys didn't have to do all this." I say, suddenly feeling self-conscious about all the work they're putting in. "I'm fine with just coffee."

Atlas turns away from the stove to glare at me. "That's exactly why we're doing this." He points out. "Because you won't do it for yourself."

I stare at the plethora of options they've somehow scrounged up while I was still sleeping. Eggs, toast, potatoes, pancakes, even fresh fruit. They usually order takeout and never keep the fridge this stocked. "How did you guys even get all of this here so fast?"

Tristan and Cyrus give each other a knowing look. "Ezra graciously volunteered to go on a grocery run last night." At says.

"You did?" I ask, glancing at him as he takes a slow sip of his coffee.

"Mmhmm." He murmurs, keeping his eyes closed. "Thrilled to be of assistance."

"Anything I can help with?" I ask, circling around the island to stand next to Tristan while he mans the left side of the stove.

He smiles down at me and hands me a spatula. "Will you keep an eye on these while I finish the scrambled eggs?"

I gave him a nod and smile to myself at the sheer normalcy of what we're doing. I wish we could stay like this. Pretending like everything's back to normal.

Once I finish plating the last of the bacon, the guys all take their seats around the dining room table and wait for me to join them.

As I approach the table, I lock eyes with Ezra and for a second I think about falling back into our old habits. But sitting on his lap right now would send him the wrong message and if I'm honest, I'm not even sure what message I'm trying to send. I haven't been here for 24 hours and I'm already confused. I can't imagine what these next few days will do to me.

I can't sit here and pretend that things between us are back to normal. But I also can't pretend I don't want them, no matter how hard I try to convince myself I can.

Waking up this morning really solidified things for me. Regardless of what's happened, I feel safe with The Reapers and if I want any chance of moving forward; I have to leave the past behind us and start over with them.

I take one of the open seats at the table and go to grab myself a plate.

"Already on it." Cy says, loading an empty plate up with a heaping mound of scrambled eggs. I try to take it off his hands, but before I can, Tristan grabs it and is already tossing some bacon on it. I sit back in my seat and watch as my plate travels back and forth between all four of them, and by the time Cyrus places it back in front of me, my eyes are tearing up so much that I can barely see what's on it.

Ezra studies me. "What's wrong?"

"Nothing." I say, swallowing and shaking my head as I try to pull back the emotion in my voice. "It's just. Um, why are you guys being so nice to me?"

"Why wouldn't we be nice to you?" Atlas asks as concern furrows his brow.

"Because I messed everything up with us." I sigh, looking at all of them as shame heats my face. "I hurt you. I blamed you. I fought with you. And I said some really awful things to you. I don't deserve any of this."

"Angel, we all made mistakes." Ezra says, watching me from across the table. "But that doesn't change how we feel about you."

"You have every reason to hate me." I say, looking directly at him as I shake my head. "And it's okay if you've moved on." I say pointedly, shift my eyes between Atlas, Tristan, and Cyrus. "You guys don't owe me anything."

"What are you talking about, Princess?" Cyrus asks. "Why are you looking at us like that?"

Is he really going to make me spell it out for them?

"I saw the girl leaving the office last night." I say with a sigh. "And it's fine. Like I said, you guys don't owe me anything. I can't be mad at you for what happened."

"Princess, we haven't moved on." Cyrus says, wrinkling his nose.

"Far from it, actually." Tristan adds as his brows harden into a scowl.

Atlas studies my face. "She was there as a result of my poor judgment, but nothing happened. She was there to keep up appearances, nothing more. All of us have been trying to deal with your disappearance the best way we could. been torn the fuck apart when you left."

"We all were." Ezra adds, locking his eyes on mine.

There's a lot more to all of this than I thought. *Have they really missed me as much as I've missed them?*

"I don't understand. If that's the case, why didn't you guys try to find me?"

"We didn't think you wanted us to." Atlas says, clenching his jaw. "We thought you wanted us to leave you alone."

He's right. When I first left them, all I wanted was to get as far away from them as I could. But now, that couldn't be further from the truth.

"If we had any idea where you really were…" he pauses, shaking his head, "we would've gotten you the hell out of there. We would've never let him take you away."

"Dimitri said that you would've known I was with Melanie. That, after they found her body, you guys would've put two and two together and knew I was in trouble."

"We knew you were staying with her." Tris offers, working a muscle in his jaw. "Well, I knew," he corrects, "b... but we had no idea there was an attack or that Melanie was murdered."

"About that." Atlas says, cutting in as he locks eyes with me. "I was going to wait for the right time to tell you this, but since it's come up, now seems as good a time as any. This morning I made a call to one of Melanie's older brothers. I wanted to offer my condolences and assure them we were going to whatever it took to track Dimitri down."

"Okay... and?" I ask, trying to decipher his unreadable expression.

"Stevie, Melanie's not dead."

What? She survived? How in the hell did she survive?

"Neither is Charles." He continues. "Somehow, they both managed to survive the attack and have been recovering in a secure facility outside of the city."

"I need to go see them." I say, glance around the table at each one of them. "Will one of you take me to go see them?"

Atlas shakes his head. "I don't think that's such a good idea, Kitten. She's still recovering and we can't let anyone from the outside world see you."

"The hospital they're at is secure. You said it yourself. And they both risked their lives trying to save me. The least I can do is come by and see them."

Atlas sighs as his shoulders slump. "Fine, I'll see what I can do. Now can we stop talking and go back to enjoying our breakfast? The food is getting cold."

EIGHTEEN

AFTER WE'RE THROUGH WITH BREAKFAST, THE conversation picks up again. Only this time, it centers on Dimitri and what's on the agenda for the day.

It hasn't even been a full day since I told them what was going on, and they have already set so many things into motion.

Last night, after I went to bed, Atlas reached out to a

member of The Council that he trusts and unofficially confirmed everything that The Mercenaries told us.

He knew I was telling the truth about what happened, but he wanted to make sure he had The Organization's blessing before he and his brothers joined in on the hunt for Dimitri.

Immediately after speaking with them, he texted Tristan and had him set up a tap into all of Dimitri's known phone lines. Apparently, Dimitri had the foresight to block his location but not enough foresight to secure his actual line. That's good news for us, because with the right conversation, they should have no problem tracking him down.

"Cyrus, Tristan, and I have set up a few meetings we have to fly out for with some of the other leaders we know we can trust. We should be back tomorrow night at the latest. You think you two can manage to not rip each other's heads off until then?"

"We'll play nice." Ezra says, glaring at me as takes a slow sip of his coffee. "Won't we, Angel?"

I bristle slightly as the images of last night replay in my head. Ezra may be acting civil towards me right now, but he's still unpredictable. I'm not sure if I'm ready to be alone with him, but I'm not going to tell them that. Dimitri has to be stopped and I don't want to keep them from doing what needs to be done to bring that monster to justice.

I'll be fine. But tomorrow night can't come soon enough.

A FEW HOURS LATER, I'm sending Alex updates and doing a pretty damn good job of avoiding the only other person in the house when I hear a knock at my door.

I look up from my phone and quickly toss it aside as I stride towards my door. I'd normally ask who it is, but I already know the answer. I slide the door open and sure enough, mister tall, tatted, and dangerous is waiting on the other side.

"Can we talk?" He asks, moistening his lips as he lets his eyes roam over my body. His expression is unreadable as ever as he leans against the threshold and holds my gaze.

"Sure." I stammer, studying him for a moment as I try to decipher what's going through his head right now.

I'm not sure why I keep trying to search his face for answers. When it comes to how he's feeling, Ezra's a lot like me. Guarded. Mysterious. Aloof. It's probably why we've never fully embraced our connection. Both of us like to wear our masks and we wear them well.

"Not here." Ezra says, shaking his head. "In my room. There's something I need to show you."

Ezra walks us to his room and holds the door open for me, watching my reaction as I step into his space. As soon as I pick up the notes of smoky lavender in the air, bittersweet nostalgia tugs at my heart.

I miss it. Who we used to be back when things were simpler between him and I. Back when I loved him blindly and didn't care what that meant for us. Back when I didn't burn the bridge we so carefully built together.

Ezra watches me as I walk through his room. Studying my face as my eyes take in each of the new pieces of art he's created in my absence. Some tilted on an easel, some lined along the walls, but most of them are stacked haphazardly on the ground in disorganized piles. The color variations are different with each one, but the overall tone is the same. Dark. Chaotic. Messy.

"What is all this?" I ask as I slowly circle around the room.

"This..." he pauses, visibly swallowing, "was my way of dealing with your absence. Every time I missed you, I let my monster take over and release itself on anyone who deserved it. These were the end results."

Jesus. There has to be at least two dozen of them. I look up at Ezra and he immediately lowers his gaze and shakes his head.

He thinks I'm disappointed. That I'll judge him for what he's done, but that couldn't be further from the truth.

Ezra isn't a bad person. He's doing the best he can with the demons he was given. He isn't perfect, but neither am I and I would never judge him for dealing with his pain the only way he knows how.

If anything, I'm sad. I'm sad that I abandoned him when he needed me the most, and I'm sad that I messed up this thing between us that was once really beautiful.

I move towards him and place my hand along his jaw, trying to convey the sorrow that my words could never fully express.

"There's something else I need to show you." Ezra says, pulling out my hold. He walks me over to an easel with a much larger canvas draped in a white sheet and tosses the sheet aside. The moment I see what's lying beneath it, tears well in my eyes.

The colors in this painting are vivid and bright, and its hyper realistic style is a stark contrast to the rest of the more abstract artwork I've seen from him before. Even without the intricate details, it's a photo I'd recognize anywhere.

It's the picture. The same one of me and Alex I found at his bedside the night I ran away.

I graze my fingers over the canvas and worry my lip as I study the bright smiles on our faces.

I remember this day. *God, we were so innocent back then.* Our mother had just passed, and Malcolm was still relatively stable. We took this the day after her funeral and we'd always laugh about how fucked up it was that this day was the happiest we'd ever looked.

"I started working on it a couple of months ago." Ezra offers, pressing his lips together in a hard line. "I know it isn't anything great, but I figured you might still like to keep it."

I turn to face him, staring at him with glassy eyes as the emotions start to overwhelm me. "Ez, this is... this is the best gift anyone has ever given me."

I wrap my arms around him, squeezing him tighter than I've ever held anyone before. He's solid and warm and beautiful and so fucking tragic and he's all mine.

"I missed you." Ezra says, breathing into my hair as he pulls me closer. "And I shouldn't have lied to you about your sister."

I slowly shake my head. His lie may have been the catalyst for why I ran that night, but I was already teetering on the edge of self-destruction. If he didn't push me over the edge, something else would've.

"I thought I was doing the right thing." He says. "Giving you the closure that you needed to move on. I didn't realize how stupid of an idea that was until it was too late."

"Like you said, we both made mistakes." I say, holding his gaze. "There's so many awful things I wish I could take back and honestly, I don't blame you for what happened last night. You have every reason to hate me."

"I don't hate you, Angel." He says, locking his eyes

on me. "I never have. Last night was an accident. I know it's hard to believe, but I mistook you for someone else."

"You said my name Ez. It's okay if it wasn't an accident. None of this has been easy."

"It hasn't." He says, shaking his head. "But it truly was an accident. I mistook you for your ghost. The same one that's been haunting me ever since you left and when I ran into you, I had no idea that you were real. I would never intentionally hurt you, Angel. You're everything to me. Always have been. Always will be."

"After everything I've done to you, how could you possibly still feel that way about me?" I ask, looking up at him. "How could you possibly still care about me?"

Ezra furrows his brow and cocks his head at me like it's the most ridiculous question he's ever heard. "You have no idea how I really feel about you, do you?"

He runs his hand down my face and I press into his touch, too enraptured by everything he's saying to think of all the reasons why this is a bad idea.

"For the longest time, my world centered on my demons." He says, holding me close as he presses my head into his chest. "They were my driving force and the only things really keeping me going. I care about my brothers, but if I'm honest, a part of me always felt like they'd be better off without me. I was too saturated in the darkness to get out, but they were still good. They tapped into their darkness when they needed to, but they never felt at home with it, like I did. That was the hand dealt to me and, mostly, I accepted it. That is until I met you."

He pulls me back and his smoky gray eyes come alive as he studies my face. He stares at me with a mixture of awe and unabashed adoration. "I don't know why you did it, or if you even meant to do it, but on the night we first met, when you looked up at me, it was the first time I didn't see the look of fear staring back at me. You saw something else in me. What? I'm not sure, but it felt good and that was... *unexpected.* After that, something inside me shifted. I found myself wanting to be different. Better. Kind. The type of man that deserves to be with someone like you. I know I'll never be a good man, a man that wants you for all of the right reasons, and says all the right things, but for you, I'm willing to try. If you'll let me."

I'M at a loss for words. I always knew he and I had this strange connection, but I never knew he saw me like that. Like this beacon of hope in his world filled with darkness.

I look up at him and for the first time since I walked through that door; I stop over thinking and just allow myself to just be present in the moment. Ezra cares for me. He wants to be better for me. And right now, all I want to do is show him how much his words mean to me.

I pull him in for a soft kiss, allowing my body to melt

deeper into his touch. He hesitates at first, as if he's a little unsure, but as our kiss deepens, he slides his hands down my back and lifts me up off my feet.

He blindly strides across the room, ignoring the piles of canvases that scatter across the floor, before slamming my back against his vast floor to ceiling window.

The glass is surprisingly cool to the touch, and little shivers run up and down my spine as our kiss gets filthier and filthier. Ezra kisses like he fucks. All brutal and rough while still leaving you begging for more.

I whimper against his lips as I claw for the hem of his t-shirt, doing everything I can to rip it off of his back. I need to feel him. All of him.

Ezra breaks our kiss, flashing me a wicked grin as he sets me back down on my feet and starts stripping the rest of his clothes off. I do the same, tossing my shirt aside and kicking off my yoga pants as quickly as I can.

"Turn around." He orders, rotating his index finger in a slow circle. "I want those perfect tits of yours pressed against the fucking glass."

I do as I'm told and am rewarded with his cock filling me to the brim at the same moment his fingers reach around and delicately circle my clit. I snap my head back as he dives deeper into me, feeling every inch of him as he forces his way in, pumping harder and harder inside of me.

I let out a deep groan of pleasure and arch my back even further as he uses his free hand to grip a handful of my hair. He pulls with just the right amount of pressure, and my entire body feels like it's on sensation overload. The perfect mix of pain and pleasure.

"Fuck, Angel." He groans. "You feel so fucking good. It's like this pussy was molded perfectly for me."

"Play with your pussy." He orders, sliding his hand out from between my legs and planting it firmly on my hip. "Show the whole fucking world how wet you are for me."

I gasp at his words as my eyes fly open and I stare out at the world in front of us. It's quiet outside, and there's no one here but us. But the sun is just starting to set and there's plenty of cars going up and down the hill. All it would take is one little glance for them to see everything we're doing and somehow, that's even more of a turn on.

I dip my fingers between my legs, working my swollen clit in slow circles as Ezra dives into me.

"That's it, Angel." He hisses, gripping the back of my neck and shoving my face forward. "Now lick the fucking glass and show them how filthy you are."

Emboldened by his words and the way he's making me feel, I slide my tongue up and down the glass as if I'm putting on the dirtiest fucking peep show they've ever seen.

I love how rough he is with me. How he's never treated me like I was some fragile, broken thing he needs to handle with care.

As our bodies continue to collide, a light sheen of sweat starts to coat my skin. I'm slipping further down the window with every thrust, but his cock is still relentless, pounding into me harder and harder while my fingers continue to circle my clit faster and faster.

He's fucking me so brutally. So damn thoroughly that my legs are like jelly and after a while, I have no choice but to press one of my hands to the floor to try to keep my balance.

Ezra swells inside of me as my pussy clamps tighter and tighter onto his dick, riding the waves of pleasure as my fingers create the perfect amount of friction against my clit. It's so good. So goddamn perfect that I nearly want to cry. The fullness of his cock. The roughness of his hands on me. The strangers that could be watching us. All of it is too much for me to handle.

Pressure builds inside of me and as soon as it hits its peak, I let out a deep groan. "Fuck, Ez. Come inside of me. Right fucking now. Come inside of me."

Ezra palms my ass and I can feel the urgency in his touch. He loves that I want his cum and he's ready to explode in me. He pounds into me, sliding in and out of my pulsing pussy with zero restraint. "Fuck, yes." I groan, bouncing against his hips. "Fuck yes."

Ezra lets out a low curse of his own and as he fills me to the brim, with the entire world possibly watching us, I have never felt more free in my life.

After we finish and have both cleaned ourselves up, I

lay beside him in bed and nestle myself against his chest. He wraps his arm around me and pulls me closer as he presses his nose to the top of my head and breathes me in. I stare up at him and as the golden sunset gleams through his windows; I feel myself melt into his arms. There are still things we need to talk about, and a lot of things left unsaid. But in this moment, feeling the slow rise and fall of his chest beneath me, I know there's nowhere else I'd rather be.

NINETEEN

SINCE THE GUYS CAME BACK FROM THEIR TRIP, I'VE noticed a change in our dynamic. We're comfortable around each other again, and I no longer feel like I'm walking on eggshells around them.

I guess it's because everything's out in the open now. I'm not hiding anything from them and they're keeping me in the loop with everything going on in the outside world. They're still hunting for Dimitri, and I'm still technically in hiding, but in a weird way, this is the most normal we've ever been.

Our days even have a routine to them now. Breakfast is always the same, with all four of them doting on me way more than they should before heading out to follow up on leads. And even though I always insist that I'm fine, one of them always stays behind to keep me company.

It's weird. We're in the same setting, with all the same players, but living with them this time around feels different. More whole and complete. Like we could really make a life out of this.

But every time I get those feelings and an inkling of happiness sets in, I can't help but feel like it's going to get ripped out from underneath me. Like at any moment, something terrible is going to happen and I'm going to lose everything all over again.

Trying to distract myself from those morbid thoughts, I grab my cell phone and shoot Alex a text as I plop myself in front of the electric fireplace in my room.

After the long shower I just had, the fire is exactly what I need to warm up again.

Stevie: How was Day 4 of captivity for you?

Alex: Boring AF. lol. How was yours?

Stevie: Surprisingly good. It's weird how normal it feels.

Alex: I know the feeling… I've been with these guys for what? Like three weeks? But it feels like I've known them forever.

Stevie: Speaking of the guys… Are you going to tell me which one you have a crush on yet?

Alex: For the billionth time. It's not like that with us. Not all of us can handle juggling as many dudes as you.

Stevie: Sureee

Alex: You're an insufferable ass lol

Stevie: And you sound exactly like Creed! Does that mean he's your favorite?

Alex: In-freaking-sufferable.

I LAUGH to myself as I shake my head and lean back into the armchair. Pestering her about The Mercenaries has become one of my favorite things to do lately. She always gets so defensive about it and for some reason, it's wildly amusing to me. It's my job as her big sister to give her shit and I like that we have something to talk about other than the danger we're in.

"What's so funny?" Tristan asks, cocking his head as he and Cy look at me from my open doorway. They must've just finished showering, too. They're both wearing nothing but boxer briefs, and I can still see tiny beads of water dripping from their wet hair.

"My sister." I say, showing them the phone in my hand for emphasis. "She thinks I'm insufferable."

"She's not wrong." Cy teases. "It's a good thing you're mildly attractive, otherwise we would've never put up with you."

I scoff at his joke, just to mess with him. "Mildly, huh? If I remember correctly, weren't you the one all over me on day one?"

"That's just because I didn't realize how insane you were yet. Once the crazy cat was out of the bag, it knocked your hotness way down."

"Is that so?" I ask, cocking my brow as I rise from my seat and stride towards the two of them. I'm feeling playful tonight, and Cyrus just made himself an easy target. "That's too bad." I say, looking up at him with a heated gaze. "I was just about to ask if the two of you wanted to sleep in my room tonight. But since you find me only mildly attractive, I guess it'll just be your brother and I tonight."

"Come on, Tris." I say, linking my hand in his as I pull him towards my bed. "Cyrus won't want to see what happens next."

Tristan stifles a laugh as I drag him to my bed and I make a show of flipping my hair as we walk away. He knows exactly what I'm doing, and luckily for me, he's enjoying messing with his twin as much as I am.

Cyrus glares at us, brooding from the doorway.

"You should probably close the door." I call out, laying Tristan flat on my bed before mounting myself on top of him. "Unless, of course, you're into watching."

Cyrus cocks his jaw as he slowly shakes his head. He looks pissed. *Good. Serves him right for teasing me.*

He reaches for the door handle, but instead of closing it, like I expect him to, he slips into the room with us and softly shuts the door behind him.

Fuck. He's calling my bluff. Tristan spots the panic in my eyes and before I can stop him, he lets out a deep chuckle.

"What the hell is so funny?" Cyrus snaps, glaring at the two of us.

Seeing the confusion on his face makes me burst into laughter and before I know it, the both of us are laying flat on the bed, cracking up.

"You guys are assholes." Cy says, glaring at us.

"Cy, I was just kidding." I say, shaking my head with a smile. "You didn't seriously think I'd force you to watch me bang your brother, did you?"

"Kinkier things have happened." He retorts with a shrug. "Besides, who said I'd have to be forced into it?"

Embarrassment flushes my cheeks as I slowly shake my head. "But seriously, do you guys want to sleep in here tonight? The bed is enormous, and this big house gets a little creepy now that there's no staff bustling around."

"I'm in. We were going to sleep outside again anyway, and the bed is better than the hard ass floor in the hallway." Tristan says, shrugging his shoulders as

"What about you?" I ask, glaring at Cyrus.

"Fine." Cy says, scowling as he approaches the bed. "But only if you're in the middle. That asshole drools when he sleeps and I refuse to wake up next to his fucking puddle again."

I AWAKE some time in the middle of the night to the feeling of heat building inside of me. I have no idea where it's coming from, but my nipples are pressing against the thin fabric of my white tank top, and I can already feel the evidence of my arousal pooling between my legs. I shift slightly and immediately feel something hard jump to attention between my ass cheeks. I snap my eyes open and turn to glare at Cyrus. He's sleeping soundly, but somehow I've managed to press my ass firmly into Cyrus' lap while we were sleeping. I'm still wearing my pajama shorts and he's still in his box briefs, but if the fabric wasn't there, he'd probably already be inside me.

How fucking embarrassing.

I gave him so much shit about not finding me attractive, and here I am, sleep-humping him against his will.

I slowly inch off of him, careful not to wake either of them, but as soon as we're apart, I feel a hand grab my hip and shift me back into place. "Stay." Cy groans, pressing sleepy kisses down the back of my neck.

I swallow and slowly arch my back until my sensitive clit hits his hard bulge. I swing my hips forward and do it again, hoping that Tristan can't feel my subtle movements.

I know it's wrong. I know Tristan is right there, and at any moment he could wake up and catch us, but somehow knowing he's there makes this even hotter.

Following my cue, Cyrus presses his swollen cock harder against me and my hips instinctively grind faster against him. His hands roam my body, and the anticipation building inside of me slowly sends me into a frenzy. "Fuck." I hiss, gasping as his fingers slip between my legs and he rubs a single finger against my swollen clit with slow, soft circles. "Tris is right there." I whisper, turning my head to face Cyrus. "What if we wake him up?"

"You already have." Tristan says with a chuckle, grabbing my jaw and turning me to face him. "But don't think you have to stop for me." He says, rubbing his thumb across my bottom lip as I sink my teeth into it. "I love watching how your body responds, no matter which one of us is touching it."

"What do you think, Princess?" Cyrus asks, grazing his lips up and down my neck. "Do you want to give my brother a little show?"

I nod my head and a part of me can't believe I'm

agreeing to this, but just the thought of Tristan watching me come all over his twin's cock does something to me.

"A nod isn't good enough." Tristan says, gripping my face as he slowly shakes his head. "Not for this. If you want me to watch you get fucked, be a good little pet and speak."

"Y-yes." I stammer, equally outraged as I am turned on by the command.

"Yes. What?" He challenges, licking his full lips as he watches one of Cyrus' hands slide up my body and begin fondling my breast.

"Yes. I want you to watch me, Tristan."

"Good fucking girl." Cyrus hisses, teasing my sensitive nipple under my white tank top with one hand while sliding down my sleep shorts and panties with the other.

Tristan watches my face, mesmerized, as Cyrus pushes me forward and slips his hard cock inside of me. His hungry eyes are locked onto mine, watching every flinch, every eye roll, every single response as his brother shoves his enormous cock inside of me. "You love big cock, don't you, pet?"

I nod my head as Cyrus' strokes intensify and his hips slap against my soft ass.

"Say it." Tristan orders.

"I love big cock." I groan, watching his heated expression as he watches me get fucked. He really does love this. I glare down at Tristan's cock and can see the visible outline of his shaft still tucked into his boxer briefs. Fuck. Would he let me suck his cock right now if I asked? Just the thought of feeling both of them inside of me, filling me so fully, has my mouth watering. I swallow as I lick my lips and Tristan immediately takes notice.

"What do you want, pet?" He asks, cocking his head as he studies my face.

"Your cock." I moan, trying to keep focus as Cyrus lifts one of my legs up and continues his delicious assault. "I want your cock filling up my mouth."

Tristan licks his lips as he slowly strips off his boxer briefs. I snap my head down and my eyes immediately widen.

Fuck. He's so big.

Wasting no time at all, I bend forward and take his cock into my mouth. It feels impossible at first. It's thick, too thick. But as my jaw relaxes into the stretch, I take him in deeper and deeper.

Cyrus grips tightly onto my ass and soon the three of us fall into a steady rhythm. With Cyrus' cock filling my pussy at the same time as Tristan's cock fills my mouth.

"Fuck." Tristan groans, as I continue to jam his cock deeper and deeper into my throat. "Cy, you have to feel this. Her throat is fucking magic."

The next thing I know, I'm being flipped around, with my back towards Tristan and my eyes on Cyrus. Cy lets out a low curse as I slide my wet mouth down his shaft. His hands dig into my hair as he guides my movements, and I shift my focus back to what Tristan is doing behind me.

Instead of entering me right away, Tristan slides my ass up until it's aligned with his face and starts devouring my ass. Licking and lapping at my sensitive flesh like he's fucking starving and I'm the first meal he's had in weeks.

We go on like that for hours. Me trapped in between them while they stimulate my body in every way possible. Licking and sucking. Touching and fucking. The twins are greedy for me and they can't get enough.

I'm like their own personal sex toy.

It's degrading. It's filthy. And it's fucking amazing.

TWENTY

Sitting alone with your thoughts has a way of putting things into perspective. And last night, while I was once again throwing myself headfirst into the search for Dimitri instead of spending time with Stevie, I realized something. I'm actively avoiding her.

Two days ago, it was supposed to be my day with her, but instead of following through with it, I handed it off to the twins and made some piss-poor excuse about how there was somewhere else I needed to be. *There wasn't.* I just didn't want to be alone with her.

Maybe it's my way of punishing myself for what happened.

She's assimilated herself back into our lives in no time at all, and while I'm happy that she's mended her relationships with everyone else, I don't think I deserve the same grace.

I failed her.

There's no other way to put it than that. She was out there suffering while I was drowning my fucking sorrows away in our club, feeling sorry for myself. I should've known that Dimitri was after her. I should've done more than just sat on my ass. I don't care if she insists nothing happened. I know that bastard, and I know he would love nothing more than to cause her pain.

As if my masochistic thoughts have lured her here, Stevie walks up and joins me in the kitchen. She breezes past me, seated at the kitchen island, and heads straight for the fridge. "Do we have anything sweet?" She asks, tilting her head slightly as she places a hand on her hip and assesses the contents of the fridge.

"I don't think so." I say, shaking my head. "I can go pick you up something?"

Stevie turns to face me. "Really?" She prods, holding my gaze. "Don't you have more work to do tonight?"

I shake my head.

The hunt for Dimitri is still going strong, but now

that we've gotten three of the other West Coast syndicates to join in on the search, the workload's been lighter. "I'm free to go wherever you need me to."

Stevie's eyes light up with excitement as she stares at me. And all I can think about is how badly I miss her and how I'll do anything I can to make her happy.

"You definitely shouldn't have said that." She jokes, narrowing her eyes at me. "Because what I really want is a giant snickerdoodle cookie from café au lait."

I let out a laugh. "That's a thirty-minute drive."

"That you used to do every time I closed." She adds with a smile. "Take a drive down memory lane."

I smirk at her and slowly shake my head, trying best to disguise the pain in my eyes.

She has no idea how often I drove past that coffee shop while she was gone. No idea that I shut myself off from the rest of the word and threw myself into the only places that reminded me of her. There and Hell's. I was a fucking wreck when she left, and I'm only slightly better now.

"Fine." I agree, holding her gaze. "If it makes you happy, I'll get you an entire box of them. But, with one stipulation. You're coming with me."

Her eyes go wide as she stares at me. "Seriously?"

"Yes, seriously. You can stay in the car while I run inside. The heavy tint will keep you fully concealed. Unless, of course, you want to stay here."

"Are you kidding?" She asks, cocking her head at

me. "Of course I want to come. I've been going crazy being locked up in here."

"Good. Now go get changed." I say, eyeing her pajamas. "I'll be waiting for you in the garage."

THE DRIVE DOWN to the city is quiet, save for the sound of Stevie's knee bobbing up and down. I can't tell if it's nervousness or excitement running through her veins, but either way, it feels good to have her at my side again.

"This is so weird." She says breathlessly as she eyes the passing city streets leading us towards Café au lait.

"What is?" I ask, cocking my head at her.

"Us. This. Being here, of all places."

I know exactly what she means, but I dig deeper anyway. "Why is that weird?" I ask, cocking a brow.

"You're right." She says, shaking her head. "Weird isn't the right word. More like, nostalgic. Yeah, being here with you is nostalgic."

I nod my head in agreement and slide my eyes back to the road. She has no fucking idea how nostalgic this feels for me, too. But it feels a hell of a lot better now than it did when I was doing this drive alone.

"You know, I always wondered what it would be like

to get closer to you. To go beyond the friendship-that-was-more-than-a-friendship thing we had going on."

I cock a brow in surprise. I never knew she felt that way. "Why didn't you try to get closer?" I ask. "Every time we toed that line, you were always the one to shut it down first. Why is that?" She knows what my initial hesitations were, but I haven't heard hers.

"Because I was scared." She confesses, moistening her lips as she looks at the window. "Alex and I were planning on leaving this town, and I knew that if I got close to you, it would be impossible to leave you behind."

I nod my head in understanding as I park the car a few spaces down from Café au lait and shut the engine off.

"And what about now?" I ask, turning to face her.

"Now I know I was right to be scared. You are exactly the kind of man a girl would change her plans for."

I pull her in for a kiss because I can't fucking deny myself anymore. She tastes like a second chance. Like she's washing away all of my mistakes with the swipe of her velvety tongue.

As we mold to each other, I can feel all the dark shit in my soul evaporate. My guilt. My sadness. All of my fucking frustration. *Gone.*

She deepens our kiss, climbing over the center console to plant her soft body firmly on my lap. My cock jerks in surprise and she lets out a little giggle as she pulls back and smiles at me. "Someone missed me." She teases, wrapping her arms around my neck.

"Kitten, you have no fucking idea." I lower my seat, and pull it back, to give us more room while Stevie licks and nibbles at my neck like she's a rabid fucking animal.

Once I'm laid back, she slides her hands down my stomach and reaches straight for my cock, squeezing the shaft hard as she lets out a little moan. She grips onto the waistband of my joggers and when she pulls it down, my cock practically jumps out at her with excitement.

Her eyes widen in surprise and she lets out a gasp before snapping her head up to look at me. "Do you have any reservations about me riding your cock right here, right now?"

I sink my teeth into my lower lip and bite down hard as I slowly shake my head.

Fuck no, I don't.

"Good." She says, shifting her body up as I help her slide her panties out of the way. "Because I'm really tired of waiting for you to make the first move."

I hold Stevie's hips in place just above me as she grabs the head of my cock and aligns it perfectly with her pussy. "Is that where you want my cock, Kitten?"

She nods her agreement and looks at me with lust-crazed eyes. "Give me." She says as her brows furrow in frustration.

"Only if you ask nicely." I tease, shifting my hips to glide my cock up and down her wet pussy.

"Please, Atlas?" She asks, looking up at me with fire in her eyes. "Will you please let me bounce on your cock?"

I release her hips without warning and as she slams down my cock; she throws her head back with a loud moan.

Our bodies clash into each other and neither of us can seem to get enough. The car is bouncing and the windows are fogging, but it's as if we've been transported into another world where it's just her and I.

"I fucking love you, Atlas Cole." She groans as she bounces and swirls her hips mercilessly on my cock.

I pull in for another kiss, greedy to taste her mouth as her confession touches a deeper part of my soul. I thought I lost her. I thought we were doomed.

"I love you too." I breathe back as she continues to fall apart on top of me. "I always have and I always will."

TWENTY-ONE

Stevie

I'VE NEVER LIKED THE SMELL OF HOSPITALS. THE STERILE furniture, the chemically clean scent, All of it reminds me of the times when I felt the most alone. It's a different hospital and a different room, but somehow it still feels exactly the same. *I shouldn't be here.*

"Maybe we should come back later?" I ask, worrying my lip as I glance over my shoulder at the room down the hallway. "She just started feeling better a couple of days ago. I don't know if she's even up for visitors."

"She cleared it with her doctors yesterday, P." Cyrus huffs as he scrolls through his phone. "Quit making excuses."

"She's fine, Baby, " Tris adds, latching his eyes on me, "and she's expecting you."

Great. They're double-teaming again. Only this time is a lot less fun.

It's the first time they've let me leave the house since I arrived and the security precautions they've taken to pull this off are pretty insane. I haven't even been able to breathe without at least two of them flanking my sides.

I won't lie. The built in security detail hasn't been as hard to adjust to as I thought it would be. I guess there's some comfort in knowing the fact that it's not me they don't trust this time. *It's Dimitri.*

"I think I should just wait a little longer." I say, stalling. "Atlas isn't even here yet."

Cyrus and Tristan give each other a look, but they say nothing. *Judgy dickheads.*

They're seated next to each other in two of the dark leather chairs lining the wall across from me, and when I'm not looking, I can feel their eyes on me.

Their concern would feel sweet if I didn't already feel so damn suffocated. I know it was my idea to come visit her, but now that I'm actually here, all I want to do is go back home.

Ezra shifts in his seat beside me and studies me with that unreadable look of his. I give him a look back that screams, "get me the fuck out of here", but he just averts his eyes and sinks deeper into his seat. Looks like I'm facing this hurdle on my own. *Figures*.

"How is she?" Atlas asks as he walks up to join the four of us. He had a followup meeting with The Mercenaries that he couldn't miss, but he made it here in good time.

"I don't know." I say numbly, rubbing my nose as I stare through the window outside of her private suite. "We haven't gone in yet."

"I see." He says, taking a seat beside me and settling into the cheap vinyl seat.

I feel uneasy. Like my stomach has been twisted into a tight knot and no matter how hard I try to loosen it, all of my efforts only make it worse. I knew coming here would feel like this, but I forced myself to do it, anyway. I owe this to her. To both of them, really. But facing them feels like such a big hurdle.

I glance at Atlas and study his features. The cool, collected display he presents is comforting and I find myself wanting to lean on him, trying to steal some of that confidence for myself. "I didn't expect it to be this hard." I say, trying to search for the right words. "It's my fault she's in there. She must hate me."

"Everyone made mistakes." He says, shaking his head. "Melanie included. And you probably aren't the only one feeling like you're to blame. You should talk to her. I can walk you there, if you want?"

Why does he always seem to know the right things to say?

I give Atlas a nod and he links his hand in mine. We get to the window just outside of her room and I pause.

"She looks tiny." I say, squeezing his hand harder. *And dull,* I don't add. Nothing like the ferocious woman that always intimidated the hell out of me.

"She lost a lot of blood." Atlas says, clenching his jaw. "But she's a survivor."

"And smart as hell." I add, with a sad smile. "It's a good thing she and Charles played dead when Dimitri's men came to wipe out the survivors."

"Yeah." Atlas retorts, rubbing his fingers against the back of my hand. "She's clever, always has been. I'm grateful she fought to save you. Otherwise, who knows what could've happened."

"She shouldn't have done that." I say, shaking my head. "She barely knows me. Why the hell would she try to save me?"

"Why don't you ask her yourself?" He suggests, looking through the window. "She wants you to come in."

I spot her smiling at me through the window and instead of stalling any longer; I bite the bullet and walk through the door.

"Hey." I say, taking a seat in the chair furthest from her.

"Jesus, Stevie." She says with a laugh. "I know I look like shit right now, but I don't bite."

"Sorry." I say, moving to slide into the seat closest to her. "I don't really know how to act right now."

"Me either." She admits. "But I'm glad you came."

Silence falls between us, and after a few awkward minutes, Mel breaks the silence. "Okay, clearly we're both shit with words, so let's just get this over with, yeah?"

"I'm sorry." We both blurt in unison as our brows furrow in confusion.

"What do you have to be sorry for?" Melanie asks, looking at me like I've grown a second head. "I'm the one that let that asshole in."

"No." I say, shaking my head. "He tricked us both. I'm the one that should be apologizing. This would've never happened if I didn't come to you for help."

"I'm glad you did." She says, shaking her head. "It made me realize that I never gave you a fair chance. You're surprisingly cool for a fiancee stealer."

I laugh. "Fake fiancee stealer." I tease.

"Same difference."

"So, how are you feeling?" I ask.

"Honestly, a lot better. Especially now that I know you're okay. Stevie, I want you to know that I tried to get my dad to tell The Reapers what happened as soon as I woke up.

I didn't remember everything, but I knew Dimitri took you and I was so fucking worried. But my asshole of a father locked me here and wouldn't let me talk to anyone. The only person I've seen beside him and my brothers is Charles."

"It's fine." I say, shaking my head. "He was just trying to keep you safe."

"It's not fine." She bites out, suddenly getting her full gusto back. "Sorry," she adds, shaking her head, "over the years I've made a lot of excuses for my father and turned a blind eye to some of the awful things he's done because he's family. But he crossed a line. You were with Dimitri for days. I can't even begin to imagine what kind of awful things he put you through."

I look away, unable to hide the raw emotions threatening to surface. I pushed my time with Dimitri so far back into the recesses of my mind, I never want to think of them again.

"It doesn't matter." I say, shaking my head. "I'm safe now and so are you. That's all that matters."

"You're right." She says. "I have a lot of things to make amends for, but I'm thrilled that things between you and me are good."

"Me too, Mel."

"Hey stranger." Melanie says, directing a smile towards someone standing by the door. I turn to follow her gaze and spot Atlas leaning against the doorway. He and her have a history I don't think I'll ever quite understand, but the pang of jealousy I used to feel towards her isn't there anymore.

"You're alive." He notes, crossing his arms over his chest.

"Surprisingly." She jokes, shaking her head. "You know, your girl here put up quite the fight before I passed out. I'm sure if she didn't, Dimitri would've tried to finish what he started. She saved my ass."

"Hey." I hear another voice say, as someone else walks up behind Atlas. "She wasn't the only one who helped save your ass."

I burst out of my seat and rush towards Charles, pulling him into a tight hug.

"Should I be jealous?" Atlas asks, directing the question at Melanie as the two of them watch me nearly tackle him to the ground.

"Maybe?" She teases. "I mean, he did save us, and you know how us girls love our knights in shining armor."

"Hey." I say, smiling at her. "I'd be hugging you like this too if you weren't stuck in a hospital bed."

I release Charles and see that he didn't come empty handed. He sets the greasy paper bag of food down on the tray beside her bed and Melanie's eyes light up.

"Don't say shit." She growls, practically ripping open the bag. "I almost died. I can eat as many fucking cheeseburgers as I want."

I like this new Mel, and I can almost guarantee that Charles has everything to do with it.

As Melanie digs into her burgers and falls into a meaty cheesy bliss, Atlas and I turn to leave. It was good to see her, but we still have some important things to take care of. Namely, the bastard that we're all searching for.

"Hey Stevie," Melanie calls out, catching Atlas and I just as we are about to walk out the door. "When you find that motherfucker, make him suffer for me, will you?"

I flash her a devious smile as I give her a firm nod.

He's going to pay for everything he did to us.

I guarantee it.

TWENTY-TWO

Stevie

I TAKE A DEEP BREATH AS I GIVE MYSELF ONE LAST ONCE-
over in the mirror. The past week has flown by and we're
still no closer to finding Dimitri. Somehow, he got wind
of his unofficial blacklisting and has been doing everything he can to evade capture. *We'll find him.* I'm sure of
it, and tonight, I'm excited that they're finally letting me
in on some of the action.

"You almost ready?" Cyrus asks as he gently knocks on my door.

"Yeah, just about." I reply as I finish lacing up my boots. I've learned through trial and error that it's always good to have shoes I can run with if needed.

Cyrus steps through the door and gives me an appreciative once over. "You look good, P." He says, cocking his slightly with a grin.

"I don't want to look good." I say, sliding the billowy fabric of my red dress up and revealing the loaded holster around my thigh. "I want to look intimidating."

Cyrus laughs as he shakes his head. "Fine, then let me correct myself. You look like a badass that could beat the shit out of me. Better?"

I laugh. "It's an improvement." I adjust my blond wig one last time before adding a pair of aviator sunglasses to complete the look. "Thank you for letting me come with you tonight. I've been going a little stir crazy staying locked up in the house."

"Of course." He says, wrapping his arm around my shoulder. "Just make sure you keep the sunglasses on and we should be good. And for the record, we don't like having to keep you cooped up in here either. But we're still having a hard time tracking Mitri down and I don't think any of us will feel good about you being out in the open until we catch him."

"I know." I nod, trying not to get creeped out at the mention of his name.

Dimitri has become this ever present dark cloud over us. It's like he's always there, seconds away from pouring down on us, but we have no clue when the storm will hit.

Cyrus leads me out to the driveway and when I spot which bike he's pulled out of the garage I let out a little squeal.

"We're taking the freaking Ducati?"

Cyrus tries to fight the smile that tugs at his lips. "Yeah, it's a bit of a drive so I figured we could at least have a little fun with it." Cy loves this bike more than he loves most people and as much as he tries to hide it, he's totally eating up my excitement right now.

He hands me an extra helmet. "Whoa, this actually fits pretty well. I was expecting it to be too big on me."

"I, uh, ordered it a while back for you. You know, in case you ever wanted to ride with me again."

I can tell he doesn't want me to make a big deal about it, but I have to say something. He's always so thoughtful and I want him to know how much I appreciate that. "Hey," I say, grabbing his hand before he hops on, "thank you for thinking of me, Cy. Seriously."

"It's not a big deal." He says, brushing me off with a shrug. But it is, especially to someone who grew up in a household where my needs were the last thing on anyone's mind.

We hop on his bike, and I settle against his back as he starts the engine. We fly down the hill and the ride down is as exhilarating as it is terrifying. Once we hit the freeway, I grip onto his body for dear life. I know I'm probably squeezing the life out of him, but it's as if my muscles are paralyzed in fear.

About an hour later, Cy finally pulls off of the freeway and I'm able to breathe again. Once we slow down to a normal pace, my muscles relax and my hold on him finally loosens.

"You okay?" He asks, turning his head slightly to check in on me as we pull up to a red light.

I give him a nod. "It was a lot faster than I expected."

"I may or may not have been driving a little crazier on purpose."

"What? Why would you do that?"

"So you'd squeeze me tighter."

"Dick move, Cy." I joke, shaking my head. "Dick move."

We pull up to an older single story office building with a fading exterior and the most boring boxy architecture I've ever seen.

"You sure this is the place?" I ask, hoping off the bike as I scan the barren parking lot. "It doesn't look like anyone else is here."

"I'm sure." Cy says with a nod. "Most of the people that come to this place don't want anyone to spot them, so they'll usually have a car drop them off. High stakes underground casinos like this aren't exactly legal."

"How do you know so much about this place?"

"We own it," Cy says with a shrug as if it's the most casual thing ever. He notices the look on my face and narrows his eyes at me. "What's that face for?"

"I just —. If you own this place, wouldn't Dimitri avoid it like the plague? I mean, you guys would know he was here the second he walked through the building."

Of course, Cy says with a nod. "But it's not Mitri we're looking for tonight. We're looking for his minions. Under The Organization's eyes, they've done nothing wrong, so they have no reason to hide. But under our eyes, not so much."

"I see."

"Don't feel bad for them." Cy says, taking my hand in his. "Mitri may have been the only one to harm you, but that doesn't make these men innocent. Besides, if anyone knows where that son of a bitch is hiding, it's them."

Fuck. When I told them what happened, I really wish I had told them everything. They don't know about The Zombie or the shit he did to me for the first few days of my capture. If they did, there would be an all out witch hunt for two men, not one.

I didn't tell them the full truth for two reasons. One, because I didn't want them to know I was tortured, and two, because I didn't want them to look at me any differently. I just hope that was the right choice.

Cyrus and I make our way into the building. It's been a while since I've been around strangers, but I feel a certain level of comfort knowing he's by my side. Plus, the anonymity I have with the wig and sunglasses on makes me feel unstoppable.

As soon as we walk through the doors, we're met with what looks like a small office building. The lights are off, but I can make out a handful of light gray cubicles filling the center of the large room.

"It's a facade." Cy says, pulling me towards the back of the office. "Instead of blacking out the windows and placing it in the middle of nowhere, we thought it'd be better to hide it in plain sight."

Make sense.

Cy slips out an access card, similar to the one they use for the house and Hell's, and swipes it across a small detector. The light flashes green and there's a sound of a lock shifting.

Cy opens the door, and we're greeted with a sleek set of glass stairs. It's a stark contrast to the boring beige and gray office we're leaving, and it almost feels like we're stepping into a completely different world. "After you, Princess."

Cy and I take the steps down hand in hand and when we reach the bottom, he slips his hand around my waist. "Do me a favor?" He asks, pulling me close. "Stay by me tonight. The clients that come here can be pretty entitled.

I don't want anyone getting any ideas about your importance to me."

I give him a nod and as he leads me down the final dark corridor; we round the corner and step into another world entirely.

The place screams modern luxury. All glass and chrome accents meshing with dark furnishings and plush black velvet game tables. Even the cocktail servers' outfits fit the theme.

"Nice... uniforms?" I say, watching one of the girls walk by as the crystals dangling off her otherwise nude bikini reflect in the light.

"Be nice." He says, wrapping his arm over my shoulder as he weaves us towards the bar. "We established the dress code long before we met you and the original girls had input in designing them."

He has a point. The outfits are no more revealing than what you'd wear at the beach and, honestly; their outfits are pretty hot. I kind of want one for myself.

"So what's the plan?" I ask, staring at the lines and lines of card tables.

"Well, one of his men signed up for an Omaha tournament tonight. The plan is to sit and wait until he shows his face. Then ask him a few questions."

"That's it?" I ask.

"Sorry, P. Are you expecting a little more excitement?"

I give him a shrug.

"How about I let you drive home?"

"I want excitement, Cy, not a horrific death."

"Fair enough."

We take a seat towards the back of the bar, so I can stay out of view and Cyrus orders us a couple of cocktails as I scan the crowd.

"Relax, tiger." He jokes, sliding me a mixed drink with a slice of fresh pineapple hanging on the rim. "We're just here to talk to someone."

I give him a smile and shake my head.

"You're right. It just... it feels good to be able to be doing something for a change. I know I agreed to stay out of it, but it's hard staying home and not knowing what's going on. I feel like you guys are doing so much for me and my sister. I just... I really want to help tonight."

Cy wraps his arm around me and pulls me in for a soft kiss. "You are helping, P. We wouldn't even be able to do any of this without all the details you gave us about your time with him."

I let myself sink into his hold, but in the back of my mind, I can't help but feel a little guilty. I haven't shared every detail with them.

As if my guilty conscience conjured him into existence, a man steps into the card room and my body stiffens as recognition clicks in an instant.

Fuck.

"You okay?" Cyrus asks, pulling my sunglasses

down to get a better look at me. I try to mask my reaction and avert my eyes, but I'm too slow. Cyrus follows my line of sight and, without another word, he stands up from his seat and drags me along with him.

"You know her?" He asks, looming over the man in question as he nods his head towards me.

The Zombie's callous eyes skim over me before looking back at Cyrus. "Nope."

Fucking liar.

Cyrus scoffs. "I'm not sure if you heard me." He snaps, raising his voice even louder. The entire room comes to a standstill, and it's as if all of their eyes are on us. "I said. Do. You. Know. Her."

The Zombie sucks his teeth as he glares at him. "I believe that's a question you should be asking her."

Cyrus lets out a laugh, as if they're just having some friendly banter, but I can tell by the look in his eyes that this is anything but friendly. Without a warning, Cy's fist goes flying and smashes into the side of The Zombie's face with such ferocity, I literally hear his cheek bone crack. The Zombie crashes to the ground and when Cy backs away, I'm half convinced the fight is over, but soon realize he's only preparing himself to throw another hit.

"Cy don't." I say, catching his arm and trying to hold him back. "He's not worth it."

"He's not." He says simply, looking deeply into my eyes. "But you are, P. I know exactly who this motherfucker is and what he likes to do. He's not going to get away with what he did to you. Not tonight."

In an instant, Cyrus is on him, pounding his fists into him like nothing I've ever seen before. The Zombie tries to hit him back, even lands a couple of cheap shots, but Cyrus is better. Faster. He's fighting him like he's been training his whole life for this. And as strange as it sounds, watching him defend my honor like this pulls at my heartstring in a way I didn't expect.

I haven't had someone protect me so ferociously like this since my dad. And somehow, I know that if he were here, and he saw this, he would be just as fucking proud of Cy as I am.

Cy continues to beat the shit out of him and it doesn't stop until his own security team finally steps in to separate them.

When he's finished with him, The Zombie is barely moving and, to add insult to his injury, Cy spits on him right before he has his security team drag his barely conscious body to the back.

"Let this be a lesson to anyone thinking of laying a finger on our fucking Queen. Your punishment will be swift. Your punishment will be brutal. And your punishment will be bloody."

After the fight, Cy doesn't speak to me. Not when he drags me out of the casino. Not when he walks to his motorcycle. And not when he helps me get on it.

It isn't until he parks the bike at the top of this huge

peak overlooking San Francisco that he speaks to me again. "Why didn't you tell us?"

I kick at the loose gravel underneath my boots. "I was trying to protect you guys."

"Keeping things from us doesn't protect us. It hurts us. You need to tell us everything. That's how we build trust."

"I'm sorry, Cy." I really am. I saw the pain on his face when he realized we knew each other. It physically hurt him to find out like that, and it wasn't okay for me to keep it hidden. "I should've told you everything from the beginning."

"You're right." He says, working the muscles in his jaw. "You should've. We have to trust each other, P. Especially in our world. People are constantly going to be trying to rip us apart, but we have to be stronger than that. From now on, no more secrets. No more lies."

"Okay."

"Come here." He says, outstretching his arms towards me. I hesitate, if only briefly, because I honest-to-god don't think I deserve it. Cyrus is consistently kind to me and I feel like I find a way to make him regret that kindness. I don't want to do that anymore. Not with him. Not with any of them.

"Princess." He says sternly, glaring down at me. "If you're going to have a fucking pity party, have one in my arms. It's cold up here and I need to remind myself that

that motherfucker can't get to you anymore. That you're with me now, and that you're safe."

And with that, I practically throw myself into his arms. I have a stupid pattern of punishing myself every time I make a mistake, as if my misery will somehow remedy the situation. But in order for me to grow, I have to learn from my mistakes, not fear them.

TWENTY-THREE

Stevie

IT DIDN'T TAKE LONG FOR EZRA AND ATLAS TO GET THE information we needed out of The Zombie. For someone so enamored with torture, he sure didn't last very long once he was on the receiving end. It couldn't have been more than a couple of hours from the time they got him into the basement to the time they called us to let us know the job was done.

Forty-eight hours later and here we are, summoning everyone to Hell's Tavern, with a location in hand and a room full of people ready to give Dimitri exactly what he deserves. Most of the faces I don't recognize, but the ones I do, make my heart squeeze. Melanie's here and she brought Charles along with a group of four guys I can only assume are her brothers. Alex is here too, seated in a booth with The Mercenaries, and she's decked out in all kinds of tactical gear. There's three other groups of men that I don't recognize, but if they are with us on this, then that makes them an ally.

"Thank you all for coming to meet us on such short notice." Atlas says, walking out into the center of the empty dance floor to address the room. "As you know, Dimitri Evanoff has become The Organization's most wanted fugitive, and we summoned you all here tonight because we have some important updates."

He slowly paces across the room and it's as if every eye in the building gravitates towards him.

God, he was born to be a leader.

"We know where he is," he continues, "and we know he isn't alone. So I need to warn you now that this will be a dangerous mission. He's hired one of the largest motorcycle clubs in San Francisco as his muscle and we have it on good authority that he's sleeping like a baby in their club house as we speak. Right now, he's a caged animal and he will do whatever it takes to evade his punishment. The five of us," he says, pausing to let his eyes linger on me, "are going after him tonight. For us, this is personal and we can't let his transgressions against The Organization slide. Now, I've asked you here, because all of you are the people I trust most. But if you aren't prepared to risk your life tonight, I ask that you leave now. No one in this room will judge you."

Atlas turns away, giving everyone a chance to do just that, but when he turns back and finds the same faces staring back at him, I see a flicker of emotion reach his eyes.

That's right. I think, nodding my head as he locks eyes with me. *These people will follow you into a fire and so will I.*

"Okay." He says with a nod. "Then let's get started."

<hr />

WE MEET up at a parking structure located two blocks away from Dimitri's hideout. As soon as he throws the car in park, Ezra kills the engine and the five of us slip out on silent feet. Atlas leads our pack to the rendezvous point at the edge of the structure and we wait there for everyone else to convene.

As soon as we're sure everyone's there, Tristan slides

out his phone and pulls up a diagram of the building's blueprint and forwards it to each team member.

"How are we on the alarm system?" Atlas asks.

"Disabled." Cy says, with a firm nod. "And the camera feeds are looping. No way in hell they'll see us coming."

"Good. Okay, everybody listen up. Their clubhouse has three different levels, with housing on the upper two levels and a large common area taking up the lower level. Keep this in mind as you navigate through. Our only mission is to capture Dimitri Evanoff, dead or alive, and the other people in there are merely obstacles. If they aren't trying to kill you, don't kill them. But be prepared, because chances are they will try to kill you. There's six different entry points to this warehouse, here, here, here, here, here, and here." Atlas says, pointing out the doors on the map. "Those will be our points of entry."

"That gives each of us our own way in and our own way out. Mel, you and your guys can take the North-East entrance. Creed, your team will take the North-West, while Alek and his team take the South-East. Marcos and his team will take the South-West. Emil and his team will hit the West, and my family and I will take care of the East."

"I'm taking the front." Ezra bites out. "Alone."

"That's fucking suicide." Cyrus retorts with a scowl. "You can't. It'll be the most heavily guarded, not to mention you'll have no backup if something goes wrong."

"It's the most direct route, and it'll be easier to be undetected if I slip in alone." Ez offers, shrugging his shoulders. "We all know the second Dimitri gets wind of our presence, he'll try to run. Someone needs to intercept him at the front door."

He's right. Once he realizes what's happening, that's the first place he'll run to. Someone has to be there.

"I'll do it." Atlas says, nodding his head. "If you're right, then we'll need someone that can keep him there and keep him talking. He's spent his whole life in a one-sided competition with me. I doubt he'll be able to resist the opportunity to rub what he's done in my face."

"What do you think we're walking into?" I ask, glaring up at the four of them.

"It doesn't matter." Ezra hisses, taking on a sinister grin. "Anyone who stands in our way of capturing that motherfucker is dying tonight."

WE ATTACK AS A UNIT, and we attack all at once, bursting through their doors with almost perfect precision. At first, the element of surprise works in our favor. As soon as we breach the first floor, half of the club members flee on instinct, while the ones that choose to stay and fight are put down quickly and efficiently. It isn't until we hit the second floor where the real madness begins.

Smoke fills the air as the sound of muffled violence ricochets through the thin walls. I can't even tell where the sounds are coming from, let alone who's fighting who, but it's enough to put me on high alert. I'm worried about Atlas and I hate that he volunteered to protect the main entrance, but if anyone can handle fighting Dimitri one on one, it's him.

I stay close to Tristan and Cyrus as Ezra clears each room we pass before signaling us to move forward. It's quiet in these hallways. Uncomfortably quiet. And as soon as we round a corner, we find out why.

Bullets fly towards us, and an ambush is in full effect. The twins immediately barricade me, using their bodies as shields as they throw me to the ground and pull me to safety.

"We need to move." Cyrus says, screaming at Ezra as he unloads another clip on the bastards. "There's too many of them."

I scramble to my feet and the four of us rush down the hallway. Ezra tries to hold them off for as long as he can, but once they realize we're running, they advance on us. We make it to the back stairwell and in the chaos; I fall behind. I try to catch up to them, but as they climb up, bullets fly into the stairwell and I have no choice but to climb down.

Fuck, I really wanted to be there when they found him, but the agreement I made with The Reapers was clear. They let me join them in the fight, if and only if I promised to head back to the rendezvous point if we got separated. As frustrating as it is to be on the sidelines, I can't betray their trust.

I scale down the stairs with my gun drawn and my eyes wide, listening for any signs of someone else approaching. Most of the noise sounds like it's coming from further upstairs, but I can't be too careful. All it would take is one lone straggler to catch me off guard and it would be lights-out for me.

I make it down to the first floor without incident, but the second I hear the distinct sound of a woman's scream coming from above me, I immediately turn back.

I race up the steps, taking two at a time as my adrenaline shifts into overdrive.

Where is she?

Where the fuck is she?

I pick up the sound of a stream of bitter curses and shove the second floor door open to find Melanie sitting on the floor with her back against a wall and her barrel pointed directly at me. As soon as she realizes it's me, she lowers her gun and breathes out a sigh of relief. "Stupid asshole caught me in the leg as he was hitting the ground." She explains with a shake of her head.

"Come on," I say, throwing one of her arms over my shoulder and helping her to her feet. "Let's get you the hell out of here."

After we get to the rendezvous point and I quickly tend to her wound, I know I can't stay. Alex is still in there and I know she thinks she can take care of herself, but Mel can handle a gun better than anyone I know, and she still got hurt. *I have to go back for her.* I can't leave her in that fucking chaos.

I make it back to the warehouse with record timing and decide to enter through the north-west entrance, hoping to find Alex there. The stairwell is empty, so I head straight for the first floor common room and as soon as I take a few steps inside, I hear the distinct sound of a gun being cocked.

"Hello, Kroshka," Dimitri says, pressing the hot tip of his revolver against the back of my head. "Welcome back from the dead."

"So, you've been the missing link all along?" Dimitri scoffs bitterly as he shakes his head. "I wondered how this all came to be, but I should've known. You've been dying to fuck me any way you could."

"I hate to be the bearer of bad news," I say, trying to

distract him as I slip a knife from my front pocket, "but you're kind of fucked either way. Did you see all the people that have come for you? Do you honestly think you're going to walk out of this place alive?"

"I will." He says, hissing the words in my ear. "No one's going to touch me as long as I have you as my shield."

The Reapers bust through the door and my heart leaps out of my chest at the sight of them. A light shines behind them, illuminating more silhouettes as they enter the room. It's Alex and The Mercenaries.

They look like warriors. Bloodied, bruised, and innately savage. Their wild eyes scan the dark hallway and when they finally settle on me, I see a little slice of humanity return to their eyes.

"Stevie." Atlas breaths.

"Drop your fucking weapons." Dimitri hisses as he digs the steel barrel of his gun against the back of my head. "Unless, of course, you want me to blow her fucking head off?"

"Don't you fucking do it." I say, choking back the emotion in my voice as I gaze deeply into each of their eyes. "Keep. Them. On. Him."

Indecision flashes through all of their faces and suddenly, I know what's going to happen with startling clarity. They're going to drop their guns. Because they love me and because they can't stand to watch me die.

But the second they do, Dimitri will kill me anyway.

Because he knows it'll break them and that, above everything else, was always his goal.

I can't let him hurt them like that. *I won't.*

I'm so sick of feeling like everything just happens to me. That I have no real control over anything and am constantly just reacting to everyone else.

For once in my life, I'm going to take charge. For once in my life, I will not be afraid. I may not be able to control what they do, but I sure as hell can control what I do. And I'm not letting that bastard win.

I flick my eyes over to my men and take in their faces one more time.

God, they're really going to hate me for this.

I close my eyes and clutch the hilt of the knife, feeling its weight in my hand. Before any of them can do anything to stop me, I jerk my arm up and stab it straight into my neck, slicing the blade across the center of my throat without hesitation.

I hope they understand.

I was going to die tonight, either way. At least this way, it was on my terms and I can die knowing the people I care about most are safe.

I think I finally understand what my dad meant all those years ago. Living isn't just about trying to cling on to every ounce of life you have left. It's about experiencing it, for however long that may be. And I can honestly say that the life I lived with The Reapers was a full one filled with laughs and love and tragedy and triumph.

And in my last moments, just before everything turns dark, I smile at my four brave knights and silently thank them for helping me conquer my fears and finally slay the last of my dragons.

TWENTY-FOUR

Cyrus

A GUT-WRENCHING SCREAM CUTS THROUGH THE CHAOS, echoing off the walls and filling the entire room. The sound is so primal. So fucking guttural that I can almost feel the pain as if it were my own.

It's Ezra.

He's fallen to his knees and when he snaps his head up, the emotion of his face is so raw, it almost hurts to look at it.

What the fuck happened?

I shift my gaze from Dimitri to Stevie and see the metallic gleam of a knife as it slips from her hands. She stares at the four of us serenely before her eyes roll into the back of her head and a stream of deep crimson blood seeps down her neck. The image is so shocking that for a moment, I can't comprehend what's happening. I just stand there frozen in place. I can't move. I can't think. All I can do is stare in horror as the color slowly drains from her face.

Stevie's legs give out from underneath her and when I see her body fold unnaturally into itself, I finally snap out of it.

"Cyrus!" Atlas snaps, yelling for me as he and Tristan race to her side. "Call a fucking ambulance."

I'm on it in no time. Dialing the numbers and barking out the address to the dispatcher. Chaos is still erupting around us, but with The Mercenaries containing Dimitri, and the other crews holding off his goons, we can keep all of our focus to her.

"S... she's going to be okay, right?" Tristan asks, his eyes flicking from her pale face to the pool of blood filling around her body.

Atlas finishes wrapping his shirt around her throat and grimaces. "I don't know." He sighs, shaking his head. "She's lost a lot of blood. God, where the fuck is the ambulance?"

"Why would she do that?" I ask, staring at her lifeless body. "We could've stopped him." I choke out. "We could've fucking saved her."

"She did it because she didn't have a choice." Alex says numbly as she moves to kneel next to her sister. "Dimitri was going to kill her either way. I know my sister. She did this to protect us."

Fuck. That sounds exactly like something she would do. Sacrificing herself for everyone else and not thinking for one fucking second about how any of us would deal with the aftermath.

Noticing his absence, I leave Alex, Tristan and Atlas, to tend to her wound and search the room for Ezra. I search among the bodies and find him exactly as I left him; staring at Stevie's lifeless body with a look of pure anguish on his face.

Seeing her like this is going to push him over the edge.

Ezra looks up at me before slowly dragging his eyes towards Dimitri, who is now cowering in the corner of the room where The Mercenaries have him cornered. Ezra cocks his head and as he glares at him and his eyes take on an almost feral look.

Fuck.

Ezra jumps to his feet and breaks out into a full-blown sprint, crossing the distance between the two of them in a matter of seconds. Dimitri notices his approach a second too late and his eyes widen in horror as he fumbles for his gun, but he's too fucking slow. Ezra is already on him, throwing him to the ground and kicking his gun clear across the room.

Ezra's fists start flying and with the amount of fury he has coursing through his veins, I already know Dimitri doesn't stand a fucking chance.

Ez beats the shit out of him, even as heavy sobs rake through his trembling body. "You fucking killed her!" He screams, pummeling his fists into Dimitri's face over and over again. "You motherfucker!" He shouts, screaming the words at the top of his lungs. "You fucking killed her."

He keeps screaming at him and there's so much raw emotion in his voice that everyone in the room slowly takes notice.

I've never seen Ezra cry before.

None of us have.

Ezra keeps hitting him, even as the chaos in the room dies down. Even as the medics come to rush her away. Even as the room fills with nothing but the sound of his sobs and the thud of his fits crunching against wet flesh.

He just keeps hitting him.

TWENTY-FIVE

Stevie

I AWAKE TO THE SOUND OF BEEPING. SLOW AND persistent, like a ticking time clock designed to drive me slowly into madness.

Beep. Beep. Beep. Beep.

The scent of cheap disinfectant fills the air, and as I take in a deep breath, I can almost feel the sting of the chemicals in my nose. There's a bitter taste in my mouth and when I try to swallow, unexpected pain stabs into me.

What is going on with me?

I rack my mind, trying to scour through the last few memories I can recall. But my head is pounding and everything is so muddy and vague that it's impossible to see anything clearly.

I force my heavy lids open, but the effort alone is taxing, and I only manage to blink a few times before the bright lights above me slam them shut again.

"She's waking up." Someone murmurs from above me. His voice sounds vaguely familiar, but with my head still viciously pounding, it's impossible to place him.

I feel someone brush a few stray hairs from my face, and the familiarity of it jogs my memory as dread sinks deep into my gut.

No. No. No.

I'm back in that room with him.

I try to scream out, but my raw throat only throbs in protest, and the sound that escapes is nothing more than a croak.

What the hell happened to me? Why doesn't my voice work?

Strong hands grab onto my shoulders, pinning me down with sheer brute force.

"Calm down. Calm down." Someone tries to assure me. "Everything is going to be okay."

Everything is not okay! I want to scream out as I struggle against the arms pinning me down.

I don't want to die. I'm not ready to die.

Then it happens. All the memories come crashing down on me, filling my head with images of the last few moments I remember. I stop struggling and lay perfectly still as they play through my head like scenes out of a movie. *The clubhouse. The attack. Saving Melanie. Running into Dimitri. The Reapers. The knife. The darkness.*

"What's wrong with her?" Someone asks, obvious concern laced in their voice. This time, I recognize the voice almost immediately. Ezra.

I blink my eyes open and the sight in front of me makes my heart kick out a dull thud. They're here. All of The Reapers are here with me.

Relief and love and gratitude seep into me and instead of holding it in, I let it out freely. Tears well in my eyes and as big fat salty tears start to spill over, all four of them approach my bedside.

"Hey. You're okay." Atlas reassures, as he slips his hand behind my back and starts rubbing it in slow circles. "You're okay. You're safe now."

I nod my head even as I continue to cry. I know I'm safe. That's why I'm crying. I thought I lost everyone, but somehow I'm getting a second chance and I'm overwhelmingly grateful for it.

The guys patiently wait for my tears to stop pouring,

all the while offering me comfort and whispering soft reassurances in my ear. They let me take all the time I need to digest everything that's happened.

When I'm finally ready to talk, I open my mouth but again, no sound comes out and my eyes widen in panic. The guys are on it in an instant. Tristan hands me a whiteboard and a dry erase marker while Cyrus explains what happened.

"You just got out of surgery." He offers, and my hand immediately flies to my neck. Sure enough, it's extremely tender to the touch and wrapped up in bandages. "When you sliced your throat, you cut through your laryngeal nerve and paralyze one of your vocal cords." He says. "The doctors say you'll be in recovery for at least five weeks."

Five weeks of silence? I shake my head in disbelief.

Ezra shrugs. "I'm just glad your aim was shit, and you didn't hit your jugular."

I grab the whiteboard and scribble out a message before flashing it at them.

'Dimitri? Alex? Melanie?'

"Dimitri is dead." Ezra says, holding my gaze. "You never have to worry about that asshole ever again."

"And Alex and Melanie should be on their way back any second." Atlas offers. "The doctors told us you might want to eat something when you wake up from surgery, so they stepped out to go pick up smoothies."

Together? I want to ask, but think better of it. Wilder

things have happened, and we're all kind of bonded by this trauma in a weird way.

"Stevie, there's something we want to discuss with you." Atlas says, garnering my attention. "I know, originally, the plan was for you to leave with Alex as soon as Dimitri was taken care of. But the four of us have been talking with your sister and uh…"

"We want you both to stay with us." Ezra offers, flashing me a wide grin.

"Indefinitely." Tristan adds with a nod.

"Princess, none of us can picture a life without you." Cyrus says, holding my gaze as he leans against the foot of my hospital bed. "We already knew that the first time we lost you, but this last time really drove the point home."

"Will you stay with us?" Atlas asks, linking his hand with mine. "Forever?"

Forever with The Reapers. It sounds like a long time, but when it comes to these four men that I love so fully and completely, somehow forever just doesn't feel long enough.

I nod my head softly as the tears start again and it's only then that I realize what I should've known all along.

The Reapers were never the villains in my story. And I was never theirs. We were always the heroes. We just couldn't see it clearly because of the armor around our hearts. But once we finally learned to lower our shields, we realized that we were always fighting for the same cause.

Us.

The Reapers are my happily ever after and I'll never let them go again.

EPILOGUE

ONE YEAR LATER

SLIPPING on my clothes from the night before, I blindly tiptoe my way towards the bedroom door. Sleeping here was a mistake, but thinking clearly was the last thing on my mind last night.

"Baby." A gravelly voice grumbles as the overhead

lights click on. "Just where the fuck d... do you think you're going?"

Shit. I think, turning around slowly. *There is no way in hell I'm escaping now.*

"Morning Tris." I offer with a smile, pretending like he didn't just catch me red-handed.

"Answer the question." He says, staring at me through narrowed eyes.

"Keep your voice down." I whisper, looking pointedly at Cyrus, still sleeping on the opposite side of the bed. "You know I have to go in early today. Alex is going to kill me if I'm late again."

"Bullshit." Cyrus mumbled, throwing an arm over his face. "You fucked your way to the top, princess. Not even Stevie Jr. can boss you around now."

"Fuck off." I laugh, chucking a throw pillow at his head. "She still hates that you call her that."

"Tough shit." He replies, as a lazy grin spreads across his face. "We hate that you insist on working at the club when you don't need the money."

I knew better than to let Cyrus and Tristan sleep with me last night, but after a long day, the offer was too enticing to pass up. Out of the four of them, the twins hate mornings the most. If they had it their way, I'd be securely locked up in the house with them until the sun went down. It's probably why they give me the most shit for taking my position at the club so seriously.

I've been running things at Hell's Tavern for a little

over a year now and since I took over and rebranded, the club has gained a 200% increase in revenue. Not to mention the surplus of new paying customers coming through our doors most nights. It feels good to watch the club's transformation from this seedy place no one knew anything about to one of the most exclusive clubs in Caspian Hills.

"If the owners would think with their heads instead of their cocks," I tease, stripping the sheets away and exposing their bodies to the chilly air, "they'd agree that their manager needs to show up to her interviews on time."

More business means more staff and lately it feels like we're hiring a new person every other week. Our interview process is a lengthy one, but it's part of the agreement the guys and I made when they agreed to let me take over.

I stifle a laugh as their long limbs clumsily clammer for the sheets I yanked off.

"You're going to regret that." Cyrus smirks as his emerald eyes glaze over with lust.

"Oh, am I?" I tease, knowing full well what kind of punishment they like to serve out.

"Get your ass over here." Tristan orders, his eyelids growing heavy. "Now."

The commanding tone Tristan uses sends a delicious thrill up my spine, and my resistance all but vanishes. Even after a year of living with The Reapers, they can still evoke the perfect rush of fear and excitement that makes me feel alive.

Being with both of them is like diving into a pool swirled with fire and ice. Like burning in an inferno while simultaneously fracturing into a million tiny pieces. And as much as I want to resist the temptation, I know there's no way in hell I'm getting to the club on time.

Alex is definitely going to kill me...

STAY IN TOUCH

To stay to up to date with my latest releases, announcements, and book recommendations, don't forget to subscribe to my newsletter at www.jessahalliwell.com

BOOKS BY JESSA

Fear The Reapers
Book One of The Reapers of Caspian Hills

Queen of The Reapers
Book Two of The Reapers of Caspian Hills

Wrath of The Reapers
Book Three of The Reapers of Caspian Hills

Brutal Enemies
A Dark Mafia Reverse Harem Romance
Release Date: TBD

Chronicles of The Damned
A Vampire Romance Charity Anthology
Releasing October 1, 2022

A NOTE FROM JESSA

Whew. You did it! You made it to the end of Stevie's wild ass journey. How are you feeling?

I know. I know. Crazy right? I wrote the damn thing and I can't even wrap my head around all the twists and turns that have happened here. I literally debated on doing a choose your own adventure style ending because I had way too many ideas flying in my head. But we made it and my heart is happy because our girl finally redeemed herself and got the happily ever after she deserved.

Stevie is a firecracker and I will miss her dearly. But... I do LOVE her world and who knows, maybe she and her guys will make a future appearance in my next books.

Thank you so so much for just being here and supporting me. It literally means the world to me that you've taken your time to read her story and I am so freaking grateful for all of you!

If you have the time, please do your girl a solid and leave a review so more people will take a chance on Stevie and her guys and I can keep crafting stories about badass woman and the dangerous men that love them.

See you in the next series ;)

xoxo Jessa

ABOUT JESSA

Jessa Halliwell *is a Reverse Harem Romance Author who writes about angsty, torturous love mixed with a dash of danger. She loves writing romance only slightly more than she loves reading it. She's been known to binge read novels then spend the rest of the day sulking over the massive book hangover.*

Jessa resides in Northern California with her boyfriend and her feisty Chihuahua named Juice. When she isn't writing, you can find her obsessing over her skincare routine, drinking an unhealthy amount of hibiscus tea, or probably crying over a really good book.

Follow me on tiktok: @jessahalliwellauthor

Join my Facebook Readers Groups: **Halliwell's Harem** *and* **Dark & Dangerous Reverse Harem Readers**